Best Wishes
Georgina Zellwood.

A Welcome Home

By Georgina Sellwood

Prologue

"Jimmy get the heck out of here," Michael called down from the hayloft.

Jimmy started to climb the ladder behind his twenty-year-old brother and their neighbor Juliana. Michael looked down from the top of the ladder. Jimmy knew that stern look and backed off right away.

"Get," Michael said again.

Twelve year old Jimmy got back on his bike and rode out of the barn.

Michael turned his attention to Juliana; she stood in the open outer door of the hayloft. The bright sun silhouetted Juliana in the double door. Dust motes shimmered in the air between them. He walked in the fresh pungent hay to stand beside her in the doorway. She looked up at him and smiled. His blue eyes smiled back. He reached over and moved a strand of blond hair from the corner of her mouth.

Kiss her!

His head dipped down, just a little. Would she move away? He dipped a little further. Their eyes locked. She hadn't moved. He was almost there, almost to her lips. He closed his eyes.

A rush of air and he opened his eyes.

She jumped, jumped out the loft door into the haystack below. She sat immersed in the fresh hay below.

So close and he missed his chance. He jumped into the hay beside her.   Maybe another day.

A Welcome Home

by Georgina Sellwood

Michael pressed his nose almost flat on the window of the bus. Rain made it hard to see, and the window had fogged up. He wiped the fog away with the arm of his jacket. He could tell his hometown was close. He began recognizing farms as they passed. Anticipation, like that of a child awaiting Santa's visit, built within him. The farms on the outskirts of town passed by his window some had changed a great deal during his absence. I'm coming home I've done my time, certainly applied to Michael. He had been away five long years and prison had greatly changed him.

The bus pulled into Maryville, his hometown, and Michael grew excited. In the years Michael had been away, the town had grown. Like a house that had outgrown its family, additions had been made. New houses stood at the edge of town, and a few new businesses lined the main street as well. A new supermarket replaced the feed and grain store. Tears stung the back of his eyes. He wanted his life back to normal. How would he ever make it when everything familiar had changed?

The bus stopped at the depot. While Michael waited to continue, he watched as relatives and friends greeted passengers with hugs and handshakes. Michael thought he recognized one of the young women that stood on the sidewalk from high school.

A couple of teenagers came on the bus. They wore the craziest hairdos Michael had ever seen. And the clothes they wore seemed outrageous to him. They dressed more like stage performers than the teens he remembered.

There on the sidewalk beside the bus stood a young couple probably, a mom, a dad and a small boy of about four years old. Dad bent down on one knee and talked to the boy. The boy sulked; As Michael watched he brought his head up, and then the little guy hurled himself into the man's arms. Michael found himself smiling. His father hugged him tightly. All was well instantly for the little guy. Michael had always wanted a wife and kids. Would that ever happen now?

A girl in pigtails flashed briefly through his mind.

He ran his hand nervously through his shaggy blonde hair and looked down at the brand-new blue jeans and crisp blue chambray shirt his Mom had sent him to wear home. Everyone wore faded jeans and well-worn shirts. He thought the new clothes were a dead give away about where he had spent his last block of time. He hoped no one noticed. His solemn blue eyes focused on the store window beside the bus. The prices had doubled while he lingered in prison. It cost a lot more money for a case of cola now. As he sat and waited for the bus to start up again, he felt a little overwhelmed by it all. His knuckles whitened on the arms of his seat. Life had gone on without him. How could he catch up?

The bus headed out of town. It wouldn't be long now, and he would be home. That Christmas-morning feeling came over him for a second time. It would be so good to see his mother again. He would see his little brother after school. It would be wonderful to see him too.

A popular song that played on the radio a few years ago talked about tying a yellow ribbon around an old oak tree, if the woman still wanted the man back after getting out of jail. The song went on to say, when the man got off the bus, one hundred yellow ribbons hung around that old tree. Michael closed his eyes and imagined that loving welcome. It would feel so good. He had a deep sense of sorrow over what had happened. He thought many times about reliving that day. *Oh, if he could only go back. If only.*

    No one could possibly know how depressed he felt while he lived in jail. He knew he didn't belong there; he felt totally trapped. During sleepless nights the smells and sounds overpowered him. The guards used disgusting language almost all the time. Unfair treatment became a regular occurrence. So many times his fists would ball up, and he would want to step in and right the injustice. But he knew he had to stand there with his hands rigid at his sides to prevent added time to his sentence. It was lonely, and he wondered how his Mom and brother coped with the farm by themselves. Did Jimmy need help in school? Did Mom stop drinking? Had she slowed down at all? He would soon have the answers.

    He slid to the edge of his seat and pressed closer to the window. He recognized the farms they passed now near his home. Marshall's had a new silo, and Benson's had a lot more horses than they used to. McRae's had even painted their old rusty barn and it still leaned slightly. It made him smile. On the far side of the road, he could see the freshly painted wooden fences of the Winslow Farms. There were at least ten horses in the pasture, beautiful well-fed, well-bred geldings and mares. Thousands of dollars stood in that one pasture. And Winslow Farms had many more pastures.

He could see Winslow's house a little way down the road in the distance. It was a large two storey colonial style with big green shutters, a small version of Tara, Scarlet O'Hara's home in Gone with the Wind. It was big enough to have six bedrooms. It looked freshly painted. They had a new fancy horse barn too. It must be nice to have that kind of money, thought Michael.

They had pulled up to his farm which stood just across the road from Winslow Farms. The bus driver remembered to stop where Michael asked him to let him out. His pulse raced, as he stood up to get a small bag out of the bin above his head. It contained all of his worldly possessions from prison. If he threw it over his shoulder at the end of a stick it would be a hobo's bag. The thought embarrassed him. It angered him that his life had come to this. He gave an old man who stared at him a hard look. The bus stopped and more people looked up at him as he exited the bus. His lips drew up into a thin line.

When his feet hit the soggy dirt at the side of the road he rejoiced. He'd finally come home. He planned on sprinting up the long laneway to the porch but a look towards the house made him stop. A painful lump formed in his throat as he stood in the pelting rain and looked at his Mom's property. First the lump stuck there because he felt so emotional to finally be home. And then the lump got bigger as he stood and looked at the sad state of disrepair of the entire property. It looked a little like Jed Clampett's old place, before he loaded his truck and moved to Beverly Hills. Paint peeled off the house in some places. A few shingles curled up and in two or three spots had come right off. New shingles would fix that. But where would he find the money with no job? How would all three of them make it?

As Michael started up the long laneway to the house, he saw that his younger brother Jimmy had harvested the hay crop off the front fields, although eight years younger, the seventeen year old had made an effort to hold things together in his absence. As he came closer to the house, he saw the porch railing missed some slats, and the windows needed a good scrubbing with vinegar and water. The screen door hung at a weird angle, and leaves covered the porch floor.

Any moment now he would be in his mother's arms, and he would bury his face in her herbal scented hair. He would stand there for moments holding back the tears he wanted to shed for so long. And Mom's love would surround him, and maybe it would be enough to make him whole again.

As he climbed the weather-beaten old steps on to the porch, he saw Grandpa's old rocker still there with Gram's right beside it. He felt comforted. Mom had left a faded multicolored afghan over the back of one chair; Michael picked it up to carry the beloved blanket inside with him. He hugged it to him remembering past comfort. Any moment now Mom would hear him on the porch and come running to greet him. She'd throw her arms around him, and all would be well. No yellow ribbons around any oak trees but that was all right, he guessed. He shuffled through fallen leaves to get to the door. Mom hadn't even swept the porch lately. His heart pounded as he opened the door and walked in.

"Hey Mom I'm home", he called.

No answer.

Oh boy! This wasn't good.

The front room was in total disarray. He scanned the room. Someone with a deep voice tried to sell him tires from the TV. A dinner plate and cup with leftovers from last night's dinner sat on the coffee table sending an unpleasant odor into the room. He stubbed his foot on a half empty bag of potato chips.

Totally disgusted Michael yelled, "Mom"

Still no answer!

Anger gave way to worry. She should have been here waiting for him. The uneasy feeling built as he picked up the plate and cup and headed to the kitchen. At least three days dishes lay in and around the sink. The end slices of a tomato lay on the counter where someone had made a sandwich. The bread bag lay open with the bread inside drying out. Fruit flies feasted on the moldy leftovers on the plates in the sink. Ketchup had spilled and dripped down the front of the cupboard. Michael sighed in disgust.

Where was she? This could only mean one thing.

He turned and stalked back to the living room where Mom's room stood off to the right. He pounded on Mom's door with no response, and then shoved it open. Mom slept on the edge of the bed softly snoring. One arm and one leg hung so far off the bed he feared she would fall out. Relieved he rushed over and lifted them back in for her. She stirred but didn't wake up. The room reeked of stale beer like a barroom. He pulled the threadbare blanket over her and brushed strands of hair from over her eyes. He opened her window a crack and left the room.

He became overwhelmed with a sick feeling, as he slumped on to the rocking chair on the porch. What had he come home to? He waited five long years to come home to a farm that had gone to rack and ruin, a messy pigsty, a Mom passed out cold and him a convicted felon just out of jail. This was not the homecoming he imagined for so long. He banged his fist over and over into his open hand like a pitcher warming up in his glove only harder, much harder. He didn't deserve this. He rocked the old chair back and forth in frustration.

Michael heard a car go by out on the road and remembered Jimmy would soon come home from school. He couldn't live in the house in the state he found it. Michael forced himself out of the rocking chair and went back into the house to see what he could do. He slammed things around but he made progress.

A little while later he heard the bus out at the road. By then he had found some meat in the freezer. He had supper cooking and he made a good start to tidy the house. Jimmy came in the front door and when he spied Michael, he ran boots and all and threw himself into Michael's arms. The two brothers stood locked in a huge bear hug. Both had wet cheeks when they finally pulled apart and stood measuring each other.

"Wow kid you've really grown. What grade are you in now?" Michael asked, as he held his brother by the elbows.

Jimmy straightened a little taller and said, "Grade eleven."

Michael put Jimmy in a headlock and playfully wrestled him down on to the worn green couch. They sat there for awhile talking and catching up.

"So what's new?" Michael wanted to know.

"Someone stole petty cash from the principal's office. Oh, and some kids had a contest shoplifting. They got caught though," Jimmy told him sounding disappointed.

"And um, do you remember Sadie Myers the old lady who lives in the stone house?"

"Yeah," said Michael nodding.

"Some kids say they saw her uptown at the post office in her underwear.' he confided grinning. Oh and Johnny Summers ran away, but his dad hauled him back."

"His dad still drinking?" Michael wanted to know.

"Yeah," nodded Jimmy.

"I think I'd be running away too. His dad's real mean when he drinks," quipped Michael.

Both of them looked away and stopped talking. The subject of a drinking parent was too close to home.

Jimmy changed the subject and apologized for the state of the house. He was away at a youth retreat for the weekend and came home late the night before. A youth retreat, Michael thought, it seemed strange, but just when he went to ask Jimmy about it, Mom suddenly stood and leaned in the doorway to her room.

Her tattered flannel nightgown was wrinkled under her housecoat. Her hair looked messy and dirty. She had sad dark bags under her eyes. Michael stood up, and his Mother sashayed across the room to him in her faded pink housecoat. His heart sped up as his Mom hugged him and kissed his cheek. He had dreamed of this moment so many times. But instead of the herbal scented hair he had remembered, he smelled the odor of greasy hair and stale beer breath. He drew back and crossed his arms. This was not the homecoming he wanted.

As they parted, he could see she had lost a lot of weight. She staggered a little and sat down heavily on the couch. She looked up at him with innocent doe eyes. He looked back hoping he hid the disgust he felt.

She looks so pathetic. Worse than the last time. He thought, his face grim ,his stomach in knots.

Jimmy had wisely made her a cup of coffee; he brought it to her now. She thanked him and aimed a kiss through blurry eyes at his cheek. Jimmy gave Michael a resigned look and walked away wiping his cheek. Michael lowered himself on to the couch beside her. She reached for Michael's hand, and she smiled.

Well at least she's glad I'm home, Michael thought.

While Jimmy started his homework at the kitchen table, Michael and his Mom caught up with news from town and the neighborhood. It felt good, finally sitting in this room with its worn green carpet, flowered papered walls and rustic rock fireplace.

"So Mom what's been happening?" Michael asked.

Mom's hand shook slightly as she talked in her gravelly barroom voice.

"Oh honey, you know the usual. Melanie Thomas married Jason Harper last month. Grandpa Harper had a heart attack and couldn't be there. That was sad." Mom looked miserable for a moment while she took a sip of her coffee.

"The mayor got pulled over for drunk driving."

"Bishop, is he still mayor?" Michael asked.

"Yes…his mother was caught shoplifting,"

Michael gave her a quizzical look. "That's an illness you know."

"How is Juliana Winslow?" Michael wanted to know.

"She's in a nursing program in the city."

Another sip of coffee then, "Did you know old man Morrison from west of town?"

"Yeah," Michael replied.

"Well he was out of gas in his truck so he drove the old John Deere to the grocery store and someone stole it."

"Oh man, who would do that?"

"I don't know but I heard at the café they found the rusted old tractor stuck in the mud northeast of town by the graveyard where the hydro lines go through."

"Gee, that sounds like kids."

"They found Miss Sadie Myers cat up a tree, took the fire department hours to get that tabby down. The thing was hissing and scratching anyone who came near it. They finally had to put Miss Sadie in the bucket and hoist her up to get it down."

Michael and his mom shared a laugh over poor Miss Sadie. Michael's laugh sounded foreign to him.

After about half an hour the buzzer sounded on the stove. Michael got up to finish preparing the supper he had started. Jimmy finished his homework and helped by setting the table. They called Mom to the table, and all three sat down to eat their very first meal together in more than five years. Jimmy asked if they could join hands, and he offered a brief prayer.

"Thank you God for this meal, and thank you for bringing us all together again. Amen", he prayed almost in a whisper.

As they sat and enjoyed the meal, Michael's first home cooked meal, he wondered what had happened in Jimmy's life to make him want to say prayers at a meal.

Not long after, Michael watched as his Mom decided to get up from the table. She wrapped her housecoat tightly around her and shuffled back to her room. Jimmy helped clear the table then headed off for a ride on his bike. Michael did the dishes then took a walk to the apple orchard out back of the house.

It felt peaceful back here, with just the wind gently rustling the leaves left on the trees. The rain had stopped and the earth smelled damp. When he got further into the rows of trees there was a faint smell of rotting apples that either fell on the ground, or apples pecked open by the birds. Michael thought of all the times he played in this orchard either climbing trees or chasing his little brother in and out among the trees. He ran after Jimmy just to hear him squeal with delight when Michael caught him and threw him to the ground and tickled him. It felt so good to be home. He wanted this for so long. He thought of all the work that came next to rebuild his life, a daunting task. He knew though deep inside the desire and ability was there if people would just give him a chance. Would they give him a chance?

CHAPTER TWO

Michael awoke early the next morning, as he did every morning for the last five years. He tossed and turned most of the night. Strangely, he found his old bed too soft. The "pallet" he slept on in jail had been hard and lumpy. It would take time to get used to the comfortable bed. He finished in the bathroom, then stood at his second storey bedroom window and looked across the road at Winslow Farms. As he stood there getting a grip on the day ahead of him, he noticed a bright red, new mustang pull into the driveway at Winslow's and drive up to the front of the house.

He came closer to the window to see who would get out of the car. He didn't wait long. A young woman with long blond hair stepped out. He noticed Mrs. Winslow come out of the front door and rush down the steps to meet the young woman. She enfolded the pretty blond in a loving embrace and hugged her tightly to her chest. The young woman clung to her, visibly shaking.

That's Juliana, thought Michael. She's grown up. He stepped closer to the window. The last time he had seen Juliana she was a fifteen year old girl who rode around on her horse in pig tails.

Mrs. Winslow now held her daughter away from her. She assessed her daughter quickly then hugged her again. The hem of her bright pink silk dressing gown flapped in the breeze. He couldn't tell from this distance, but it looked to Michael as if they both cried.

Michael had a big lump in his throat. Oh if only his homecoming was as loving and sweet as Juliana's. He felt a little cheated. He stood and watched a few moments more and Mr. Winslow came out. Now he hugged Juliana. Now Mr. Winslow had his arm around Juliana, and they went into the house. Michael watched as the beautiful woman, and her parents disappeared.

Jimmy's alarm went off. Michael turned and headed downstairs to start breakfast. He looked at the clock in the kitchen, and there was enough time to make bacon and eggs. He checked, and there was just enough in the fridge to make a meal for Jimmy. Michael found the bread and loaded the toaster, fried up the bacon and made up the mixture for scrambled eggs. Amazing aromas filled the kitchen when Jimmy came down dispelling the previous night's odors of stale air and rotting food in the sink.

"Hey Bro," Michael greeted him.

"How was your night?" He asked Jim.

"Good."

"What were you up to last night?" Michael asked, wanting to keep the conversation going.

"I rode my bike over to Winslow's. I've been helping out over there. Mucking out stalls and stuff."

"Oh cool. Does old man Winslow pay much?" Michael asked.

"Enough," was the answer.

Jimmy set the table, while Michael finished cooking the breakfast. Michael called Mom but she just rolled over. The two of them sat down alone. Michael with his coffee, and the way Jimmy was emptying his plate Mike guessed it was the best breakfast Jimmy had eaten in a while.

"I don't think she drank last night," said Michael, about Mom not getting up for breakfast.

"She has a bottle in her room," said Jimmy, with a mouthful of egg.

"Oh."

This was worse than Michael had imagined.

"Something will have to be done about this."

"Yea well, you can try," mumbled Jimmy, scraping his last mouthful of food off the plate.

"When does she have to be at work?" Michael asked, just as Jimmy went out the door to catch the school bus.

"Oh, Tuesday is her day off."

"She still working at the café in town?"

"Yep," said Jimmy, as he threw his backpack over his shoulder. With one last piece of toast shoved in his mouth, he ran out the door.

It took Michael the next half hour to tidy the kitchen. He left a note for Mom, borrowed her keys and took the car into town to get some groceries. He sent up a silent thank you to his mom for renewing his license when it had come due. At the end of his driveway he stopped to check for traffic and noticed Juliana's shiny, red mustang gone. Probably parked in their three car garage, he thought.

    Michael put his Mom's old clunker of a car in gear and headed left toward town. It felt really strange to drive. He made a mental note to take it easy, until he got the hang of driving again. After he drove for a couple of minutes, he rolled down the window. It felt good when the wind blew in. He noticed the tang of fresh wet fields. It smelled so familiar and so good. The sun shone this morning, and he felt the warmth through the windshield. All of these wonderful sights and smells he hadn't experienced in a very long time. It felt like today he finally came alive again for the first time in a long while.

    He tramped down a little harder on the gas as he made his approach into town. He realized, he better cool it as the speed limit changed to thirty ahead. He didn't want to attract any negative attention on his first trip to town.

    He rolled up his window and got ready to angle park in front of the grocery store in Maryville. He pulled in and clunked the gearshift into park and checked his wallet. He had a wad of cash in it, everything he earned while in prison, a big whopping two hundred and nineteen dollars for five years labor. Never mind, he thought, it felt good to have that money.

    He opened the door and stretched his long lanky legs out on to the pavement. He still wore the brand-new stiff jeans Mom bought him. He found any clothes left in his room were way too small. During the time away, he had grown up both inside and out. He appeared taller and leaner now and muscular from the hours in the weight room. His blonde hair had turned a sandy color now. As a teenage boy, highlights streaked his hair from the hours spent in the sun. His blue eyes had a cold harsh look to them. He had to toughen up very quickly, after he arrived in jail, to survive. People would notice a difference. He went in as an innocent and naïve young twenty-year-old, and now he felt like a seasoned veteran of life at twenty five.

He took a deep breath and went into the grocery store Thank goodness not too much had changed. He found the carts still in the same place. He felt a little nervous. His Mom had always shopped before. The last time he came with Mom to help her get groceries, he sat in the cart.
He made his way to the first aisle which was the fruit and vegetable section and stood and looked at everything and wondered what he should get.
Maybe he should have made a list.

He grabbed a bag of apples and a bag of carrots. He knew what to do with them. He didn't know how to prepare some of the vegetables. He made his way around the corner to the next aisle. He felt a little overwhelmed, by what looked like a mile of cans and boxes stacked high on both sides. This was harder than he thought.

He made his way down the aisle and picked up a can of this and a box of that as he went along. When he drove about halfway down, a little old gray haired woman with a slight stoop went by in the opposite direction. She steered her cart as far over away from him as possible. She had seen him but wouldn't look directly at him. She must know me, he thought. I guess I have the plague, he told himself. He felt disconcerted to have someone avoid him like that. His mood changed after that. He wanted to get home.

He hurried through the rest of the shopping, and went to check out. He stood in line behind a young woman with a toddler in her cart. The little boy ate a chocolate cookie and had managed to smear it over the bottom half of his cute little face. Michael winked at him, and the little guy smiled. A warm feeling spread through Michael, and it took him off guard. Maybe there were still some warm spots left in his hardened heart. The woman paid for her groceries, and Michael gave the toddler a two-finger wave as his mom took him away.

Michael's turn to check out came. The store owner at the till gave him a scowl, as he stood and waited for Michael to unload his groceries on to the belt. Michael had never unloaded a cart before, and the man got impatient as Michael struggled to speed up a bit. He finished ringing everything through and told Michael how much it cost. It took a minute to get his wallet out and find the right money.

Life on the outside sure held many challenges.

Michael gathered his groceries and went out and loaded them in the car. His next stop was the gas station. While he pumped his gas, a truck with a highway construction logo pulled up. An older man, with grimy work clothes, got out to pump gas and struck up a conversation with Michael.

"Nice day," said the man, as he looked Michael over.

"Yeah," agreed Michael, standing opposite the older man pumping gas one pump down from him.

"You happen to need work?" asked the man, as he rubbed one hand on his grimy work clothes.

"Yes," answered Michael. The man had his full attention now.

"We're resurfacing the road out toward Carleton east of town. Are you interested?"

"Yes," said Michael. He hung up his gas nozzle and stepped closer.

"We could use a few more men."

Michael felt the heat rise in his face.

What should he do? Did he tell the guy he recently left prison?

Michael bit his lip then plunged into his explanation.

"Mister, I need to tell you I just came out of prison."

Michael swallowed hard and waited.

That's the end of the conversation, he thought bitterly.

The man stood for a moment and gave Michael another once over. Michael stood making eye contact.

Then the construction boss asked, "Can you be on time every day?"

"Yes sir."

"Will you give me an honest day's work?"

"Yes," Michael nodded.

"You won't cause me any trouble?"

"No sir, I promise."

"OK then," the man said smiling.

He offered his hand, and Michael shook it gratefully and said, "You won't regret it, sir."

The man handed his card to Michael and he clutched it in his grip as if he feared it might disappear.

"I live between town and the construction site. Would it be possible to catch a ride with someone going by? I live across from Winslow Farms,"

"Sure, I'll pick you up in the morning and then you can arrange with one of the crew to carpool."

"Thanks, I appreciate that," said Michael smiling.

The man clapped Michael on the back, as they both went in to pay for the gas.

After he paid for his gas, Michael bought a few new clothes he would need, and then headed for home. As he drove along, he caught himself humming a song. When he realized, he smiled to himself. He had not felt this good in a very long time. Maybe everything would be all right. If he had a job it would help his Mom out a lot. And he could still work around the farm.

Michael drove home and went into the kitchen to put the groceries away. Mom sat at the kitchen table drinking coffee. Michael set the bags down on the counter and bent down to give his Mom a quick kiss. As he bent down, she bought the cup up for another sip, and then she realized what Michael wanted. She stopped to let him kiss her. Michael got a good whiff of the distinct odor of alcohol from inside the cup.

Oh, Mom what are you thinking, starting to drink this early in the day, he asked himself. To her he said "You having a bad morning Mom?"

"No, dear why do you ask?"

"You're starting to drink very early, aren't you?"

"Oh Michael, mind your own business." She said, glaring.

"Mom," he took her hand and sat down in the chair next to her. "I care about you and so does Jimmy, we want you with us for a long time."

"Well, don't you worry dear. I will be." She answered.

"They teach in AA in prison. If you drink heavily all kinds of bad things can happen and you can shorten your life span a lot." He tried to reason with her.

"Oh honey they just tell you that to scare you."

She got up and headed into the living room. Michael decided not to go after her; she was not at a point yet where she would listen. This would get worse before it could get better, he told himself.

Michael put the groceries away and tidied up the kitchen. He headed outside to get an idea of what needed done in the yard. He tackled the leaves on the front porch, a quick and easy first job. He fixed the leaning front screen door. He straightened some things left out around in the yard. He put them away in the old tool shed with the rake he used.

He headed over to the weather-beaten old barn. Its paint peeled badly and it had developed a bad southerly lean. As he walked in, the rancid smell of molded hay and dust assailed him. Animals had not used the barn in a very long time, but the faint odor of dung still hung in the air. Evening light filtered between the slats in several places on the outer wall. Barn swallows dive-bombed him briefly; he had disturbed their siesta. The barn in general had a much-neglected look to it. He leaned against a nearby timber as he surveyed the old rickety ladder to the loft, and the few bales of hay piled in one corner. He remembered a day long ago when a certain young lady had avoided his kiss in that very hay loft.

As he stood there his hand on the ancient wood, he had a brief sense of the essence of all of his ancestors, and the animals that had lived and worked in the barn. It was very brief and almost imperceptible. He couldn't remember ever feeling like this before. He stood in awe for a moment and wished someone else stood there with him to share the moment. He would have asked them if they had felt "their" presence too.

He shook the feeling off and tried to get back to the reason he had come. He accessed the tools that were still there. Surprisingly Dad had left plenty, and they seemed in good working condition. There was a mower, a rake, a wagon and a bailer, used for the haying operation. Then for the orchard, he had left an old sprayer, ladders and crates.

Just for fun Michael started up his dad's old tractor and let it run for a few minutes. It sputtered briefly then put-putted in a healthy rhythm. He couldn't let it run too long as the noxious fumes filled the barn. But as he sat there, he felt close to his father. Dad died a longtime ago, and he guessed his Mom wasn't over her husband's death. Her drinking came because of her inability to cope with the loss. Michael turned the tractor off and sat and thought about his Mother. He wondered how he could help her to get off the alcohol and get on with the rest of her life. Sadness and anger filled his heart to the point of physical pain in his chest. I have to find a way to help her, he told himself.

CHAPTER THREE

Juliana turned left into her dad's driveway. The large Winslow Farms sign stood in the grass to her right and greeted her. She felt so good to be home. Tears stung her eyes as she maneuvered the candy apple red mustang, her dad had bought for her, up in front of the porch. She unbuckled her seat belt and wrapped her suede coat around her thick middle and tied the belt.

She spied her Mother at the picture window of the living room. She struggled to get out of the car, desperate to feel her mom's loving arms around her. As soon as her feet hit the driveway, her mom ran down the wide oval steps and enveloped her in a warm hug. They both shook and cried uncontrollably.

"Honey please don't cry, everything will be all right," Mom said.

"Oh Mama," Juliana whispered, reverting to her childhood name for her Mother.

The next thing Juliana knew, her dad held her in his arms, and she cried even harder.

"Juliana what's wrong?" dad asked concern in his voice.

Mom gave her a stern look.

"Nothing dad, I'm just so glad to be home."

He would be disappointed in her, when with her Mother's help; she shared her news with him. He placed his hand on her back and accompanied her into the house.

Mrs. Winslow made all of them a cup of tea, and they settled into the comfortable chairs in front of the fireplace. The warmth permeating from the fireplace gave her comfort. Juliana sat and quietly sipped the hot tea and listened to the large oak logs crackling in the hearth. Her heart felt heavy with the news she had to deliver. She gazed at her stocking toe as she dug it into the plush oriental carpet. She avoided eye contact with her parents. Her Mother had given her a look that said, now was not the time to share her news with her dad.

Marion, Juliana's mom, chatted about events that had happened in and around town. Harvey, her dad, sat and observed his daughter in silence. When the teapot was empty Juliana asked "Would you mind if I go out to see Lightning now?" Both parents nodded.

As she walked to the barn Juliana remembered giving her horse this name, Lightning Bolt at birth. He had a Lightning bolt like blaze on the middle of his forehead. Juliana grew up on the massive farm with no siblings and her horse was her closest friend. When she needed spiritual or emotional comfort, she often turned to him for a shoulder to cry on, when her Mom and Dad were too busy. The big fella and the two boys on the much smaller farm across the road were her buddies. The boys were more like mean mischievous brothers than friends. They had played and gotten into trouble together when they were kids.

She hugged Lightning's neck; she wondered how the boys were. She thought Jimmy would be in high school, but she had no idea where Michael lived now.
A prison upstate was the last she heard. For a brief second she remembered an incident years ago, when Michael had looked down at her from an apple tree in the orchard behind his house. He had tossed apples down to her and suddenly a warm soft look had come into his blue eyes; it was momentary but powerful. It still gave her a warm glow and goose bumps.

She finished her visit with her horse, then went and looked for Manuel, the stable hand, who had lived on the farm longer than she had. She loved this elderly man now as much as one of her own uncles. He expressed surprise and delight to see Juliana. He embraced her in a huge friendly hug. Tears shone in his wrinkled, weathered eyes. Bad events had happened to her during the time spent away but Juliana knew for certain Manuel would always love her even after she shared her news.

"How are you Manuel?"

"You know I get by."

"And your wife and kids?"

"They good Miss Juliana. The boss he waits."

"Oh we'll talk later then."

***

The time sped by for Michael; his first day at work had been good and bad.

The work itself had gone well. Years in the weight room helped. The labor was easy, he hardly even felt sore afterwards. And by now following orders came natural to him. His problem would be to trust the men's friendliness toward him. "Inside," he never let his guard down. Yes he did make some friends, but he never could fully trust another person, guard or inmate, because there was always the chance they would turn on him.

Michael found out Al Barton had given him the job. He took him around and introduced him to the crew and showed him where they kept the equipment. Al explained what he expected of him. Al put him on the paving crew and gave him a broom like tool that he used to smooth the asphalt, as it poured on to the highway surface. It was long boring work, but Michael determined to tough it out.

At break time the men had tried to get him to join in the conversation, but he gave stilted one word answers. He knew this was not the way to become one of the crew, but he found old habits would die hard. He would have to work at it.

When the shift ended, Michael felt weary. The guys wanted to head into town to the bar for "a couple of brews." One of the younger men named Scott asked if Michael would like a ride into town for a brew. Michael said he couldn't go to the bar, but he would really appreciate a ride home, as it was on the way. Michael did not want to start drinking with the boys. That wouldn't get his life back on track. He enjoyed the ride home with Scott. He was friendly and personable.

When Scott dropped him off across from his driveway, Michael surveyed the Winslow yard for a glimpse of a bright red car or some long blond hair. He didn't see any, so he crossed the highway and headed up the laneway to his house. He hoped Mom had started supper because he felt hungry. He trudged almost to the porch, when the front door opened and Jimmy came out.

"Mom needs milk for the supper she's making," yelled Jimmy. He threw Michael the car keys.

"Can you go into town and get some for her? She's making your favorite "smoosh" potatoes."

"Sure," Michael yelled back.

He headed to the side of the house and warmed up the car. Smoosh potatoes were his families' name for whipped potatoes with a lot of milk and butter beaten into them. Michael's spirits rose as he realized Mom must be having one of her better days.

He backed the car around and headed out the laneway, then turned left on to the highway and headed toward town. He hadn't driven too far, when he noticed a bright red car stopped on the shoulder of the road facing toward town, it looked like Juliana's. He slowed down to take a look. Yes, someone needed some help; the open hood on the front of the car indicated a problem.

He braked into the gravel at the side of the road in front of the disabled car. His work boots crunched as he walked back to the female figure huddled under the hood. He stood back a bit, so he wouldn't startle the woman. "Can I help you?"

The blonde head under the hood came up fast. And when she turned, Michael looked into those chocolate brown, familiar eyes and long lashes that he remembered from his childhood Juliana. No pigtails just radiant long silky hair halfway down her back.

"Michael," she gasped in surprise.

"Juliana , hi."

At first Michael couldn't tell if he surprised or upset her by his offered assistance. He felt relieved when she flashed him a welcoming smile and said." This thing just quit for no reason."

She pulled her coat a little tighter as the wind swept through the trees.

"Why don't you wait in the car while I take a look?" Michael offered.

The wind whipped her hair as she walked back to wait in her car.

Michael looked under the hood but couldn't find a reason why the car quit. He put the hood down and walked to where Juliana sat and waited. She rolled the window down and greeted him with a very sheepish grin. "I think I'm out of gas," she stated looking quite embarrassed.

"You're kidding," he snapped, before he realized how that would sound. "We better go and get some gas then."

She must have thought she annoyed him because she said," I can walk back and get my dad."

"No need," he told her, "come get in my car and we can get some gas in town and bring it back."

"Are you sure it's no trouble?"

"No, come on."

He opened her car door when she hesitated, then waited while she locked the car.

She stumbled in the loose gravel in her heels. Michael took hold of her elbow and guided her to his passenger door. She had body spray on that played with his senses. Once he had her safely seated inside he sprinted in delight around the back of the car and got in. Pleasure had overtaken him. It embarrassed him to have this beautiful young woman sitting in his Mom's beat-up old car. Her car was so clean and tidy inside. But she didn't seem to mind.

    She sat a little stiffly with her hands folded in her lap. The thought that maybe it made her nervous to be alone with him went through Michael's mind. I guess this is the way many people will feel, he thought.

    He drove on toward town and tried to think of a way to put her at ease. "I saw you come home on Tuesday."

    Her eyes flew to his. Oh gee, now she will think I stalked her or something, he thought. Then he locked his eyes on the road ahead. As they continued toward town, he stole glances with his peripheral vision. She has the cutest turned up nose, he caught himself thinking.

    Juliana made a couple of attempts at conversation but by this time Michael felt afraid to say too much.

    "How long have you been home?"

    "Since Monday," Michael said, gripping the steering wheel harder.

    "It must feel great to be home."

    "Yeah," he said squirming in his seat.

    She sat quietly and played with the sleeve of her coat the rest of the way to town. He was glad she had given up trying to talk.

    They picked up a can of gas and the milk Michael had come into town for, and then headed back to Juliana's disabled car. Dusk gently fell, and the countryside looked peaceful as they passed numerous farms on the way.

The sun had gone completely down when they arrived back at the car. Michael insisted Juliana wait in her car, while he poured the gas in her tank. With the sun down a chill had settled over the land. Juliana huddled in the car. When he finished pouring in the gas, Michael gave her the sign to try the engine. It started right away. Juliana rolled down her window and gave Michael a sweet thankful smile. Michael lingered at the window. He didn't want her to leave yet.

"Thanks, Michael, you're the hero of the day."

"Oh, it was nothing," he said straitening a little taller.

"I really appreciate it."

"Well, you take care now," was all he could think to say.

"You too."

Juliana rolled up the window then headed into town.

Michael went back to his Mom's car and drove home. Juliana had certainly grown up, he mused.

***

Juliana bought the groceries in town her mother had sent her in for and went back home. As she pulled into the circular driveway in front of the house, she realized her dad had been serious when he told her he would hold a coming home party for her. Both Juliana and her mother had tried their best to dissuade him. But nothing they said had stopped him; he went full steam ahead. A catering truck stood in front of the house and a man unloaded boxes. Dad had wasted no time to set the party in motion. Juliana parked and gave a huge sigh and rested her head on the steering wheel. Oh Dad, you will be so upset when you hear my news. I really wish you hadn't done this.

She grabbed her bags out of the backseat and trudged into the house. She took the packages to the kitchen then found her mother in the dining room. Mom placed her best serving plates and crystal glasses, as well as Juliana's grandmother's silverware, neatly on the table. Marion set the table buffet style; that meant there were several guests invited. Her Mom glanced and gave her a pointed look. Juliana grimaced and helped her mother set the table. She placed the silverware in neat rows and folded the napkins. They looked like little birds, just the way her Mother liked them. There was no stopping Harvey Winslow, when he had made up his mind. Both women resigned themselves to go through with this fiasco of a party and face consequences later.

"Mom what is dad doing? This will be so embarrassing when we tell him."

"I know sweetheart but I just didn't know how to stop him."

"Gee Mom," Juliana exclaimed frustration overtaking her.

Her Mom gave her a look when she plunked the silverware down onto its place setting.

Juliana bit her lip and tried to think of something else.

Harvey went totally all out. Juliana watched as men brought in supplies and decorations. They set up a mini fountain on the table. Blue tinged water tinkled down several tiers. They hung beaded pearl streamers and strings of white lights from the ornate ceiling. They brought in trellises with flowers and netting entwined in the slits between the wood. It really seemed a bit much, thought Juliana.

It suddenly occurred to Juliana there might be a problem with what she would wear to the party. Marion went to put away the groceries that Juliana had left in the kitchen. She went upstairs to her room to find a suitable dress for such a fancy party, one that would fit her. She tried on a couple she had worn at different functions in the past. Her yellow organza looked too tight in the chest, and her blue layered chiffon felt too tight in the midriff. Then Juliana remembered a pale lilac one that had an empire waist. She desperately filed through the dresses to almost the back of the closet and found the one she looked for. She held it up in front of her and looked in her full-length mirror. Yes, it was a little out of fashion now, but if it fit it would have to do.

She slipped off the jeans and tee shirt she had worn to town, put on a slip and tried the dress. Oh, thank you. She sighed. What a relief. This one would be all right. The high empire waist and the A line of the long skirt would hide the imperfections her figure had gained, while she had been away. She pirouetted in front of the mirror in delight then dove to the bottom of the closet to find some suitable shoes.

The appointed time had come. Juliana made one last touch up to her mascara and lipstick then met her mother in the upstairs hall. They descended the long circular staircase together. Their toeless high heels peeked out from under their long gowns, as they strode down the staircase in perfect unison. Marion wore an emerald necklace and bracelet. Juliana wore her Grandmother Winslow's pearls. As Juliana slipped down the stairs silently beside her mother, she prayed.

Please Lord let this night pass by quickly. I am so sorry that Mother and I have not had the courage to tell Dad my news. This party will make things worse Lord, but I just don't know how to stop it. I know I can't upset all of the guests, but please help me to find the courage to tell Dad the truth tomorrow.

When Juliana reached the bottom of the stairs, she realized countless neighbors and friends had come to her welcome home party. Her father very proudly stood over by the fireplace in the living room and talked to the mayor. Uniformed caterers circulated with trays of drinks and canapés. A group of older women gathered around the dining room table and admired the water fountain; Juliana could see them through the French doors. Dad invited all the important people he knew, Juliana could not run away and hide as she wanted because the party was in her honor. Person after person came up to her and welcomed her back. They all asked many questions that she didn't want to answer. She tried her best to be polite and answer them if she could or put them off if they became too personal.

"How are you Juliana?" asked the mayor sideling up to her.

"Fine." Juliana answered in a stilted voice.

"It's good to see you home."

"Yes," she answered looking around for a way out.

"How is that horse of yours doing?"

"He's fine." She said getting desperate to get away now.

She just wanted, with all of her heart, for this night and this party to end.

Finally, just after ten, Mom asked the caterers to put out the sandwiches. There were trays of veggies, fruit and cheese as well as a ton of desserts. While everyone ate Juliana saw her chance and grabbed an old shawl out of the closet by the back door and went to the horse barn. Navigating the semi-dark yard in heels challenged her, but she made it to the barn with a sigh of relief. It was dark inside the barn; Manuel must have called it a night because darkness greeted her when she stepped inside. Juliana grabbed a flashlight from a bench just inside the door and made her way to Lightning's stall. Once inside, she hugged his large neck. He blew out his breath and stamped one leg in welcome. She found the peace and love she had needed all evening. She knew she couldn't stay long, but it felt so good just to feel the warmth of Lightning's body infuse hers. It comforted like a loved one's embrace. She kissed Lightning on his long warm neck wishing him a silent good night before leaving to return to the house. After replacing the flashlight she left the barn, latching the door. She turned and walked right into Jimmy. They startled. They didn't expect to see each other in the shadowy darkness. She recognized him as the teenager from across the road.

"Jimmy, hi, what you are doing here?"

"I work here now for your dad sometimes after school. I just put some tools away in the shed, and I was going to head home. I'm sorry if I scared you," he apologized.

"It's ok." She reassured him, "How is your Mom doing?"

"She's the same," he answered with a teenager's bluntness. "I'm glad you're home."

"Thanks. It's good to be home." She had started to shiver.

"You'd best go in. I'll see you again soon." He told her as he got on his bike that leaned against the barn. Then he became a shadowy figure that streaked up his laneway toward the porch light his mother had left on.

CHAPTER FOUR

Michael watched in his rearview mirror, as Juliana's mustang sped away towards town. The car ground into gear and lurched onto the road, when he stepped on the gas. He felt all lit up inside. He smiled, when he became conscious that this feeling was really happiness. He never experienced happiness quite like this before.

He pulled into the laneway and drove the short distance through the hay fields and parked the car. He grabbed the milk and headed in through the back door. The wonderful aroma of his mother's cooking filled the kitchen. Mom stood at the sink and drained the potatoes; she must have noticed him drive in. Michael gave her a kiss and set the milk down on the counter beside her.

"Would you call your brother for me please?" Mom asked.

"Sure."

Michael found Jimmy in the living room.

"Come on Jimmy supper's ready," he said roughing Jimmy's hair.

When Michael went back to the kitchen with Jimmy, Mom asked, "What took you so long in town?"

"I helped Juliana Winslow get her car back on the road," Michael explained, "She ran out of gas on her way into town. So I picked her up and helped her get a can of gas."

As the three of them sat down, Michael's senses filled with the savory aromas of his favorite foods, roast beef with gravy and cream corn wafted from his plate.

Once again Jimmy insisted on saying a blessing before they ate. Both boys attended Sunday school, but their attendance fell off before Michael went away.

"Since when did you get interested in church and praying?"

Jimmy explained. "I told you I've been working over at Winslow Farms. Well, I started to attend youth group with Juliana shortly after you left, and I have gone since then. I really enjoy it. There are about ten of us who go, and when Juliana starts to come again that will make eleven. Maybe you could come too."

Michael didn't think he was ready to be out in any group just yet, so he said, "We'll see." His faith had become shaky in the last five years.

The topic of conversation turned to other issues then. All three of them savored the fabulous meal. They enjoyed spending time together again after so long. The boys insisted Mom sit and put her feet up in the living room after supper, while they cleaned up and did the dishes.

When they finished, Jimmy took off on his bike to go work. Michael put on a warm jacket and sat in the rocking chair out on the front porch for a short while. Despite the chill, it felt good to be outside in the fresh air. A night owl hooted his gentle cry from the trees to the west of the property. Bats flew around and looked to find their night prey. There are many mice in the orchard out back, thought Michael, you should try out there.

He watched as Jimmy reached the barn across the road and parked his bike against the barn before going inside. The solitude here felt wonderful, everything was so calm and peaceful when compared with what he had lived with for so long. The noise became

unbearable at times. The inmates cursed
,snored, and men screamed out in the throes
of bad nightmares. The guards shone a light
on him numerous times in the dark as they
did their head counts.

Michael shivered; it really felt too
cold out here to sit any longer. It was so
good to have a warm haven to go into. It
might be humble, Michael thought, but it
was home. He spent the rest of the evening
with his mother on the couch and watched
TV. He put his arm around his mom, and she
snuggled into his shoulder. They had never
sat like this before. He enjoyed the warmth
and closeness. Michael suspected Mom had
more than just cola in the glass she sipped
at, but Michael refused to think about that
tonight.

***

Juliana awoke the next morning to the
sound of birds chirping on the roof outside
her window. She rolled over and snuggled
deeper into the warmth under the covers. As
her eyes opened, she noticed dust motes
gently falling through the sunlight. It
streamed in through a crack in the velvet
and the lace curtains on her floor to
ceiling windows. She had slept late, she
chided herself. Her mind drifted and she
tried to choose whether to come awake or
drift off again. It was utter luxury to
just lie here in this pleasant place
between one state and the other. No real
demands on her right now, except this
urgent need to use the washroom.

*That settled it, a very full bladder
was not about to go away.*

After she finished in the washroom,
dressed and showered, she headed downstairs
to see if Mom was ready to have a sit down
with her father. She found her mother in

the solarium fussing with her many tropical plants.

"Good morning, sweetheart," her Mom greeted her.

"Morning, Mom," Juliana answered.

"How was your night, dear? Did it feel good to be back in your own bed again?"

"Yes, it feels good to be home," she replied.

She could tell her Mother wanted to avoid "the subject". She didn't want to tell her Father the news.

"Honey, there are bagels and cream cheese if you'd like some for breakfast."

"Ok, thanks, Mom, but when will we talk to Dad?" she asked, trying to set a time and get this big horrible meeting over with. Marion still stood and fussed with the cactus on the window ledge.

"I really don't know if now is a good time. Couldn't we just wait a few days and enjoy having you home first."

"Sure, I would love that, but won't it make everything worse when Dad does find out. Won't he be even more upset that we didn't tell him right away?" Juliana wondered.

"Well, you are probably right dear, but it would just be so nice to put it off a few more days." Mom bargained.

"OK, whatever you think is best." After all Mom did know Juliana's father best, and if she thought it better to delay talking to him, then Juliana would enjoy a few more days of peace and tranquility. It was just the whole mess weighed on her conscience, and in some way she thought it might be better to have it all out in the open. Have the big blow up and get it over with. And maybe come up with a plan of how, as a family, they could deal with everything. Juliana knew how she wanted to deal with the situation, but to persuade her mother and father her idea was the best way to handle it, might prove to take much convincing. This whole problem really upset her, and she felt as if she had no one to turn to. Marion's avoidance technique made the whole thing more stressful for Juliana.

    Juliana had often heard her mother quote Scarlet O'Hara from Gone with the Wind 'I'll think about that tomorrow' and knew to pursue this now would be fruitless. She gave her mom a one-arm hug and a peck on the cheek, and headed to the kitchen to find the bagels and cream cheese, and maybe something nutritious like an orange.

    As she had so many times in the past, she took her troubles to her four legged confidant, Lightning. After eating half a bagel and some grapes, she grabbed an apple out of the frig and took it out to Lightning. The big bay gelding was glad to see her, and she hugged his neck and had a good cry. She silently mulled over her concerns and hugged her confidant's neck tightly.

    As the tears subsided she verbalized some of her feelings to her best friend.

    "I feel so bad about leaving nursing school. Leaving was the last thing I wanted to do. But I can't continue. So here I am again, back at home at the mercy of my parents. I have no other choice. I am really going to need them, Lightning. Thank goodness Mom seems to understand; considering she knows the trouble I am in she has been very good to me."

    Lightning neighed out a warning, when someone came into the barn. Juliana straightened up and brushed away her tears.

She turned to see it was wonderful old Manuel going about his many chores. He greeted her in Spanish as he passed by the stall. She wished him good day and set out to go back to the house. A warm feeling infused her. Spending time with Lightning and seeing Manuel had eased her troubles; at least for the moment. As she crossed the yard on the way back to the house, she noticed the school bus at the end of the driveway picking up Jimmy from the farm across the road. Jimmy had seen her and waved. She gave him an enthusiastic wave and silently wished him a good day at school.

She grabbed a coffee and headed to the solarium. While sipping her coffee Julie still had Jimmy on her mind. Julie remembered the time while Mike was away in prison. I tried my best to help Jimmy, she thought. Mike left him with a lot on his plate. His Mom was very little help. I thought if I got him out to bible study it would help. His Mom wasn't too keen on that. But he did come out. He was a little younger than the rest of us, but as my guest the others let him come. The Mexicans were a big help during apple picking, after I explained the situation he was in. Carlos the boss stood up for Jimmy when that buyer from the city tried to offer a low price for the apples. I guess the guy saw a kid and tried to take advantage.

My dad was good to him too when the tractor broke down during haying. Come to think of it my dad needed that hay to feed his horses for the winter. He wasn't really any big hero saving the day or anything. Well, I did my best until two years ago when I left for nursing school.

. It had been a few days, and Juliana tried to think of something a little different to do. She felt not really bored, maybe just restless. She found Mom in the kitchen rummaging in a cupboard.

"Mom would you like to come with me across the road to visit Mike's Mother."

Julie's Mom stopped what she was doing to say," Gee honey, I can't today. I have to bake pies for the party at the hall."

"Oh right, I forgot. Do you need my help?"

"No, you go on dear and get some fresh air."

"OK, if you're sure."

"Yes, go." Julie's Mom said, waving a tea towel at her.

Juliana put on her fall coat and scarf and went across the road to Janet Ardath's farm. She knocked on the door, and waited a few moments for Janet to answer. She came to the door in her housecoat and looked a little disheveled. But when she saw who stood on her front porch she threw the door open wide and welcomed Juliana with a huge smile.

"Juliana, come in, come in."

"Hi, Mrs. Ardath I hope you don't mind, I just thought I would come for a quick visit."

"Oh of course, I'm so glad to see you. How is your nursing school going?" she took Juliana's coat and offered her a chair in the living room. Juliana neglected to answer, as Janet busied herself putting the coat away.

Juliana sat and waited in the cozy little room, while Janet went to get her a coffee. The room looked a little untidy, but after all Mrs. Ardath worked, Juliana told herself.

"How are your Mom and Dad, Juliana?" Janet asked, as she gave Juliana her coffee and offered her a cookie.

"They're fine. Mom would have come with me, but she's baking pies for the social at the community hall tomorrow night."

"Oh, I'll have to drop over and see her one of these days."

"She'll like that," Juliana said, noticing a beer bottle under the sofa.

"Did your Dad get enough hay for the horses?" Janet asked.

"Yes, I think I heard him say he is all set to feed them for the winter."

Juliana searched her mind, then remembered the Ardath's and the Winslow's had an agreement, the Winslow's bought all the hay the Ardath's could grow each year. This helped the Ardath's to keep going after Janet's husband had passed away.

"I guess your apple pickers will arrive soon."

"Yes, it could be any time now."

Juliana smiled remembering each year Janet hired migratory workers from Mexico to help get the apple crop off to market. The workers when they came took over the property. They set up tents with kerosene heaters to keep warm, and the overflow set up bedrolls in the barn. They would be there a week or two to pick the apples and sort them ready for shipping. Juliana remembered as a child sneaking over in the evenings after supper to play with the Mexican children.

"We became pretty good at sign language didn't we?"

"Yes and broken English and Spanish." Janet smiled.

"The Mexican kids sure loved the old swing set by the back door, didn't they?"

"Yes and you and my boys loved playing hide and go seek with the Mexicans."

"The more who played the more fun to hide,"

Juliana smiled as she remembered, one year the Spanish kids got in a heap of trouble for running through Janet's vegetable garden. She was sure the kids couldn't understand what Janet yelled about, but the broom in her hand sent them scurrying in all directions. She hid in the ditch out at the road for about a half hour with Michael; until they were sure Mrs. Ardath wouldn't find them. The light had faded by then, and she went home and left Michael to face his mother's wrath on his own. In many ways, they had a wonderful childhood together.

Mrs. Ardath and Juliana spent another cup of coffee discussing the latest news from town, before, Juliana got up to leave. Janet rose and followed her to the door; the two women shared a warm hug. Juliana noticed how thin Janet had become.

As she walked down the long laneway toward Winslow Farms, she thought about how much fun she and Michael had as kids, and what a good husband and dad he could have been. It made her heart heavy to think any possibility along those lines was gone now, when her secret came out. The fields on either side of the driveway lay barren and her life felt barren too. God would have to sustain her through the years ahead. The bible said "He would not forsake her," and she would put it to the test during the next few years.

CHAPTER FIVE

    Michael loved the early mornings. He was the only one awake. He sat at the picture window and looked out at the barren hay fields at the front of the house. They reminded him of a man's head with a close haircut. The welcome aroma of coffee steamed from the cup he cradled in both hands. The ceramic cup warmed both palms. Soon his Mom and Jimmy would get up, and the tranquility would disappear. He sat and thought of a little red mustang stranded at the side of the road, and a beautiful young woman called, Juliana. Tears momentarily stung the back of his eyes. Dry tears he refused to give in to. The false accusations years ago caused his life to become a difficult climb uphill.

    He thought of the many things he wanted in his life that were not possible now. What woman would want to settle down with him and have a family? His future held ridicule. Could he subject children to that? People believed if a jury of his peers found him guilty then he did it.

    Oh how wrong they were.

    He wished he could talk over these fears and problems with someone. He learned long ago his Mother could not be that person. When she got too much to drink, she would blurt out family secrets. He remembered Juliana and his brother Jimmy were his confidants when he was younger. That took place when they were kids, but he was an adult now with adult problems. He knew it wasn't right to expect Jimmy, who was still a kid at seventeen, to shoulder his adult problems. This left Juliana. When they were kids, he acted like an annoying older brother, but always there for the other two. They counted on one another to keep secrets and take each others part if needed. At twenty-one he considered Juliana an adult. Would she want a friendship after so long?

    He thought she seemed friendly enough the day her car broke down. But maybe, she only needed his help that day. She seemed eager to talk though. Well this line of thought would get him nowhere, he would just have to see how it went the next time he saw her.

    Jimmy's alarm went off upstairs, Michael could barely hear it. He swallowed the last mouthful of his coffee and headed to the kitchen. The alarm signaled him to grab his lunch and head out to the end of the lane and wait for his ride to work. As he came back through the living room his Mom came out of her room, blurry eyed but awake. He kissed her cheek on the way by.

"You OK Mom, you don't look so good this morning." Michael asked concern in his voice.

"Of course I'm fine, son."

"You gonna make Jimmy some breakfast?"

"Yes dear." She gave him a dark look and went to the coffeepot.

Good, he thought, Jimmy would get a hot breakfast this morning He grabbed his work coat and hat from the front closet and started toward the road. As he walked between the misty hay fields out to the highway, he thought of how he and Scott were becoming friends and smiled. He talked a lot now on the drive to work.

As Michael stood patiently and waited at the side of the road in the chill morning air. He saw Juliana come out of the horse barn riding Lightning. He waited to see if she would wave. It delighted him when she did. He smiled and raised his hand to wave back and suddenly Scott pulled up. He got into Scott's warm vehicle and heard gravel kick up as they sped away.

***

Juliana rode out along the grassy ditch. Lightning wanted to run, but she kept him at a leisurely walk. She enjoyed poking along and admiring the huge oak trees that grew between the fence and the highway. The century old trees fascinated her. Many of their leaves still lay in the ditch; the ones the wind hadn't managed to scatter across the fields.

Stately old sentinels, she mused.

Lightning fought the bit; he wanted a good run but Juliana kept him at a slow pace. The sun felt warm on her back. As she passed under one of the huge trees a squirrel took offense and chattered at her.

It's ok, she mused. Your acorns are safe.

She came upon the construction site and saw the flagman with his bright outfit warning motorist to slow down. She scanned the men working but didn't spot Michael. His Mom had mentioned he worked with this crew.

Then suddenly it happened! The side of the hill on the other side of the road gave way. A ton of sandy, damp dirt cascaded down onto the workers below. Juliana shouted but it was too late. She spurred her horse along the ditch, when no traffic came; she crossed the road and quickly dismounted. It was the strangest thing, when the dirt came down she saw it take three of the workers and spin them off their feet. It laid them sideways into the hill and buried them in the side of the mound of disturbed dirt up to their shoulders. She saw three heads and shoulders sticking out of the hillside, like levers on three slot machines. She found Michael and instantly knelt in the dirt beside him. She would find out later it was Scott that came running up to her.

"Call 911," she yelled franticly.

"Al called them, they're on the way," Scott reassured her.

"I'm a student nurse," she explained, taking a breath to try to stay calm. "Make sure the men are all able to breathe, and have the boss take a head count to be sure no one is totally buried."

She focused on Michael's blue eyes; she had watched him as she spoke and determined his breathing looked shallow, but adequate. She tried to take the fear out of her voice as she spoke.

"I'm here Michael, I won't leave you. You're going to be fine." All of her training kicked in. "Are you hurt anywhere?"

"I don't think so," he choked out. "I feel like I'm crushed though." She saw the weight of the dirt above him made it hard for his lungs to expand enough to get air. She had to use the pulse in the side of his neck, but she determined his heart was racing, but didn't appear in distress. Scott came back to let her know he had accounted for all the men.

She asked him to stay with Michael, while she checked the other two men. Their co-workers worked to dig them out. They had exposed half of their chests, and they had wrapped something around one man's bleeding head. The ambulance roared up then, so Juliana left the two men to the ambulance attendants, and she went back to Michael. Scott and another co-worker had begun to dig him out. She sat in the dirt, with Michael's head in her lap, as they worked to free him. Al came and explained they had big equipment, but he said they didn't dare use it. It was just too dangerous; they could do damage to the men, or they could bring the rest of the hill down on all of them. Juliana took her scarf off and wrapped it around Michael's neck to help keep him warm. She hoped none of the men would go into shock. She didn't know what broken bones they might have under the mountain of dirt? As she cradled Michael's head in her lap, worried, she silently prayed.

***

Michael tumbled, before he knew it, he careened off his feet. A ton of dirt swallowed him. When the hillside had stopped shifting he couldn't move anything but his head. Trapped! For a split second he panicked. He found it impossible to expand his chest, and this gave him the urge to gasp for air. It felt like he would drowned He struggled to free himself, but of course he couldn't. He heard Juliana's voice. Call 911. He closed his eyes and struggled harder to get free, but it was fruitless. Moments passed, then Juliana came down in the dirt beside him, he could see her face. Relief flooded over him; if he died, he wouldn't be alone. He could hear her say, "I'm here Michael, I won't leave you. You're going to be fine." He tried to get a grip on his breathing many small shallow breaths eased the strain. His eyes locked on Juliana's face as she continued to assess his condition. He heard Scott's voice briefly, and he knew Scott would get him out. Juliana left then to check on two other men. He tried to keep still and concentrate on his breathing, while Scott and another co-worker named Tony worked to remove the dirt from around him. He heard Al's voice, and then he heard the ambulance come. He closed his eyes and concentrated on the sound getting closer. He felt like a baby whose mother had wrapped too tightly. And like a baby he wanted to scream in protest.

Scott patted his shoulder then, "Are you ok, buddy?" he asked, a mountain of concern in his voice. Michael nodded his head. "It'll take awhile, but we'll get you out," Scott reassured him.

"Thanks," Michael whispered. He closed his eyes again and prayed, and then Juliana came back. She knelt down in the dirt beside him again and cradled his head in her lap. Oh, that felt so good. It was harder and harder to hold his head up. Juliana wrapped something around his neck then. He hadn't realized it but he felt gradually colder and colder. His ball cap fell off while he tumbled. He felt Juliana absently smooth his hair. He wondered if she realized she was stroking him. An image flashed through his mind then of long ago, when his dad had been alive. He was just a kid. In the evenings Mom would sit on the couch and watch TV, and Dad would lie down on the couch beside her with his head in Mom's lap. Mom would stroke Dad's hair, just the way Juliana caressed his. He couldn't explain how good it felt. The most wonderful soothing feeling spread through him. It helped to keep him from thinking about the cold, or how hard it became to breathe.

Juliana finished her prayer and went over the protocol she had learned in nursing school. She hoped she had done everything she should. The paramedics had the other two men loaded in the ambulance, and one came over to make sure Juliana had everything under control until they came back. He insisted she get off the ground for a minute, while he put something under her to so she would be up off the cold ground.

"Hemorrhoids," he whispered in her ear.

"Thanks," she whispered back.

She sat quietly and talked to Michael while the men switched places, and Tony and Scott took a rest. She checked Michael's arms as they became exposed.

"Nothing broken good," she sighed with relief. His breathing improved too.

The paramedics left a spare blanket. As more of Michael's body became unearthed, she covered it to avoid exposure and shock setting in. After what seemed like forever, they finally had Michael free. Juliana held Michael's hand as the paramedics loaded him into the ambulance.

"Can she go with him?' Scott asked from beside her.

"Oh, my horse," she gasped.

"It's ok, I had one of the men take him home for you." Al explained, from the other side of the gurney.

"Jump in let's go," commanded the EMT.

Juliana called her parents when she got to the hospital. Her Dad offered to come and get her when she was ready to come home. Once Michael settled after a thorough exam by the emergency room Doctor, Juliana said her goodbyes and Michael thanked her profusely.

She patted his shoulder and suggested he try to get some sleep. He smiled and squeezed her hand as it lingered on his shoulder. When his eyes drifted shut, Juliana tiptoed out.

★★★

The next morning Juliana felt out of sorts with herself and with the world. She sat with a coffee in the solarium; she found it peaceful here among Mom's flowers and plants. She liked the way Mom had a seating area set up with a round glass table and four chairs at one end next to the windows, the perfect place for morning coffee. The sun shone in, in all of its glory, and the air held the humidity and warmth of the Amazon. With all the ferns and tropical plants it looked like a jungle too. Juliana absently watched the horses romp in the paddock nearby. She remembered a look Michael had given her in the ambulance. She could see in his face he still held some of the fear from earlier. There existed an element of relief too. He gripped her hand tightly. She gave him a reassuring smile. Their eyes locked as the EMT checked blood pressure and Michael's other vitals. As she sat now with her coffee in her hand, she became conscious that she was very fond of Michael. For moments yesterday she had been aware they could have lost him. And now she understood they had forged a deep bond in their childhood. Like a big brother, she told herself.

 She watched as her father came out to the paddock to feed the horses. He used the forklift on the tractor to fork a large bale of hay over the freshly painted fence. Then went in and broke the bale up enough so the horses could eat. The horses came at a gallop and settled around the mound of hay.

 Heaviness settled over Juliana. She had to tell Dad her news, and she had to tell him soon. This holding back bothered her. She loved her Dad so much; she ached inside, because she knew her news would hurt him. Better to have it out in the open and deal with it. Her Mother's insistence that they wait, killed her. She bowed her head and prayed. Please Lord help all of us to deal with this situation. Give me strength to cope and wisdom to know what to do. If I ever needed you, Lord, it is now.

***

    Michael woke up the next morning and felt like a mountain had fallen on him. O right it had, he said to himself and chuckled at his own little joke then he stopped abruptly. It seemed like every inch of his lower body hurt, some parts worse than others. He remembered the Doctor telling him yesterday, he was lucky to be alive. If all the dirt had landed right on top of him, he might have suffocated. The aerated dirt saved all three men from certain death, because they rolled and tumbled with the cascading earth.

    He smiled. Juliana had grown up to become a mature, self-assured young woman. He saw her praying, and understood she was still spiritual. Her beautiful brown eyes had locked on his face, and he knew for that time at least, she was there for him. It didn't mean she would always be there for him, he told himself. After all he was still a convict and she came from a very rich and influential family in the community. Her parents never did approve of Juliana's friendship with him and his brother Jimmy. He always suspected that she snuck over to see them. A longing took over his heart that he couldn't describe.

    The Doctor came by later that morning to tell Michael he could go home. But he must take it easy for a few days, and he could go back to work next Monday. His Mom and Jimmy came to pick him up in the afternoon after school. They both gave him big hugs, both so glad he could go home. They were all tired, they had spent half of the night before at Michael's bedside. They ate supper in the hospital cafeteria, and picked up some pain medication the Doctor had recommended. Very weary and very sore

Michael let his Mom drive him home. He was anxious to get home where there was a chance to see Juliana again soon.

CHAPTER SIX

The day had finally come, Marion had finally agreed. They had put off telling Harvey long enough. Mom went to get Dad, and they were to meet Juliana in the living room. Juliana stood upstairs in her bedroom and nervously combed her hair one last time. Sad, tired eyes met her in the mirror. She knew this would be one of the worst days of her young life, and she could not avoid it. Because of events that happened five months ago, she could not turn back.

Juliana wasn't innocent in all of it, but she carried the total burden and the consequences alone. No choice in the matter what so ever. She knew a tear had escaped and left a trail down her cheek. She brushed it away and took a deep breath. Her chest felt so tight it hurt to breathe. Her only consolation was her Mother had not rejected her. She had welcomed her home and promised to face Dad, with Juliana, to try to work out a solution together. Dad would be angry and hurt, and she couldn't think of a way to soften the blow.

Suddenly, she heard a truck start up in the yard below.

Why would Dad leave? Had Mom gone ahead without her and told him?

She ran to a window where she could see who climbed into the truck. It was Marion, her mom, in the driver's seat and she pulled the truck over in front of the barn door.

What on earth! Had she told Dad? Did he have a heart attack?

Then she saw Manuel, the stable hand, emerge and help Dad into the passenger side of the truck. Dad with his arm around Manuel's shoulders limped to the Chevy.

He couldn't walk on his own. Juliana dropped the hairbrush and flew through the house. When she reached the front door, the truck drove out of the driveway. Manuel still stood in the middle of the yard, she ran to him.

"Manuel what happened?" she gasped, out of breath.

"The Boss, he kicked by bad stallion," Manuel explained.

"Was his leg broken?" she asked, wringing her hands.

"I don't know," he shrugged.

"Was it bleeding?"

"Not sure. Maybe under he pants." She realized Manuel had reverted to broken English in his excitement and distress.

"It's ok, Manuel," Juliana said, touching the gentleman's bent shoulder.

"I'll call the hospital in a while and let you know how he's doing."

This could not be happening!

This was not fair; she finally had her mother talked into sitting Dad down and telling him her news. And the next thing she knew Dad left for the hospital. Juliana kicked the dirt and paced back and forth between the house and the driveway. After a while she realized how cold she had become. With a sigh of exasperation, she went back into the warm house and did some housework until enough time had passed to call the hospital. When she talked to her Mom she found out Harvey broke his leg and would be in the hospital for awhile. Mom said she would call when she was ready to come home. For a brief moment, Juliana had a vision of hog-tying her dad to the hospital bed and telling him there. But of course that wasn't possible. They didn't want anyone overhearing.

In their small town her news would spread through the whole community quickly. Better to keep the news within the family as long as possible until the secret came out.

★★★

Michael tried to take it easy for the first day or two after the accident. By the weekend he had a case of cabin fever, still a little stiff and sore; he asked Jimmy if he needed any help to muck out stalls at Winslow Farms on Saturday morning. He felt relieved when Jimmy invited him to come and help. He noticed Jimmy had been sullen since he had come home on Friday night from school.

As they worked together, Michael decided to see if he could find out what bothered Jimmy.

"So, how is school going?" Michael started. He hoped to get more than a one-word answer.

"Fine."

Well he knew something wasn't fine, so he tried again. "You keeping your grades up?'

"Yep."

This obviously wouldn't get to the problem. He had to take a more direct approach.

"What's going on at school?" Michael said hoping to get to the source of the problem.

"Nothing."

OK, that was enough, thought Michael. "Jimmy I know something is bothering you. Please tell me what it is."

Moments ticked by, while in the stall next to Michael, Jimmy shoveled dung and straw into a wheelbarrow.

Oh boy I've done it now, thought Michael, now I've made him mad, and he will clam right up. He knew Jimmy had always been a deep thinker. Something would happen in Jimmy's life and it would be a week or two before Jimmy would be ready to talk about it. I should have remembered how it is with him, thought Michael. Michael stood and leaned on his shovel and watched Jimmy. He pondered what he could possibly say to get Jimmy to talk.

Jimmy walked away to get the water bottle he had left on the bench inside the barn door. Michael watched as he took a swig. OK, I guess now is not the time, Michael realized. He put his mind back to the job at hand.

Michael spread new straw on the floor of the stall, and then Jimmy suddenly cleared his throat and said in a teenager's crackly voice.

"They think I took Hal's wallet."

Michael almost gave himself whiplash his head came up so fast. "What!"

"You heard me; the teacher thinks I took Hal's wallet." Jimmy had turned and glared defiantly at Michael.

"Why would they think that?" asked Michael "Hal's your friend, isn't he?"

"Yes, we've been friends since he moved here in kindergarten," said Jimmy, still glaring.

Michael shook his head in disbelief. "This doesn't make sense, Jim," said Michael, his forehead wrinkling in consternation.

"Oh it does to them; they found his wallet after two days when they searched all the lockers." Jimmy added sarcastically.

"What do you mean? Where was it?" Michael asked, incredulous.

"They found it in the bottom of my locker in with my stinky gym socks." he said wrinkling his nose. He remembered the disgusting smell when they pulled it out and started waving it at him.

"Ah gee Jimmy." Michael said, sounding disgusted.

"You don't think I took it, do you?" Jimmy said defensively, his voice high-pitched and distressed.

"Well if they found it in your locker." Michael stated and shrugged.

Jimmy stood with a hurt look in his eyes, defiantly staring at Michael. He grabbed the horse that belonged in the stall he cleaned and shoved him in, locked the stall, then turned on his heel and left.

Michael stood there still and leaned on his shovel in disbelief. Could Jimmy have taken the wallet? The Jimmy he knew as a kid would never have taken the wallet. But he didn't know what Jimmy would do now; they lived apart a longtime. The kid sure looked annoyed when he stomped off.

★★★

Juliana woke up Sunday morning to the sound of truck doors banging shut in the yard below her window. Her dad had come home. She rolled on to her side and knew there would be a flurry of activity downstairs while Mom got Dad settled in. She had planned on going to church. It was her first Sunday back home, and she wanted to see all of her old friends. She would have to find out if Mom needed her to stay home with Dad.

As it turned out Marion happily stayed home to fuss over Harvey. She reassured Juliana it was fine for her to go to church.

★★★

Juliana backed her little red car out of the garage and headed down the highway toward town. As she passed the spot where her car had broken down, she smiled to herself. Michael was always so kind and obliging. It felt good to think prison hadn't taken that away from him. He seemed sullen and a bit distant, but underneath the old Michael still existed. At least she hoped so.

She pulled into the church parking lot and parked in the space beside the Ardath's beat-up old car. Mrs. Ardath spoke to Juliana briefly then left. Her heart sped up, maybe Michael had come. When they were kids, Michael and Jimmy were always in church.   She was proud of Jimmy. It had taken a little coaxing on her part, but he had joined the youth group and had developed a strong vibrant faith in the past few years. She felt disappointed when she entered the church and found only Jimmy in the pew. She took the empty seat beside him and visited while they waited for the church service to begin. She told Jimmy about her Dad's accident, and asked him how Michael was doing. Fine, he told her. By his demeanor she could tell something bothered Jimmy. After church, she asked if he would like to go for a soda with her.

    She hoped she could help with whatever bothered him. They sat in a booth and sipped sodas and made eye contact over their tall soda fountain glasses.

    Juliana got right to the point. "You don't seem like your old self today Jimmy." She stated. She hoped he would open to her.

    Jimmy's mouth closed in a hard straight line and his eyes misted. She waited while he struggled, she could tell he tried to decide if he should confide in her or not.

    She reached out briefly and touched Jimmy's hand. "You don't have to tell me, but I want you to know, I am here for you."

    Her kindness overwhelmed him and tears swam in his eyes. She didn't want to embarrass him, so she tugged his hand "Come on. Let's get out of here." Jimmy leaped to his feet and waited in the car while Juliana paid.

    She drove the car a short way out of town and parked at the side of the road. Jimmy had recovered his composure by then. He sat and played with the leaflet he had brought home from church. "They think I stole a wallet," he blurted out, hurt and anger in his voice.

"What happened?"

"They found Hal's wallet in my locker," he said, barely above a whisper, unshed tears evident in his voice.

Juliana shook her head in disbelief. "How could it have gotten there?"

"I don't know," Jimmy said. One lone tear escaped his tear filled eyes and ran the length of his face to his chin. He brushed it away hoping Juliana hadn't noticed.

"Well someone must have put it there," she reasoned.

"Yea but who?" asked Jimmy, turning in the passenger seat to gage Juliana's reaction.

"Well it had to be someone in the school," stated Juliana, knowing that wasn't going to be too much help. "Is there someone at school you can talk to about this?"

"Yea Lenny, my best friend, he might be able to help me figure out who would have done it." Jimmy's face brightened. Juliana could see that now he had a whole new resolve.

He hugged her and thanked her for believing him and helping him to figure out what to do. Juliana drove him home knowing he could go to school Monday with a plan. He wouldn't have to go back feeling guilty and defeated.

CHAPTER SEVEN

Sunday evening, Juliana stepped out of the horse barn into the gray light of dusk. Lightning was fed and bedded down for the night. The yard lights spread a soft yellow glow over the ground toward the house. As she started across the yard, she noticed Ardath's porch light come on, and Michael come out his front door to sit on the porch. She changed her mind about going into the house and walked toward Ardath's. Michael noticed her as she crossed the highway and waved a greeting. She smiled returning his salute and walked a little faster.

"Can I get you a coffee?" Michael asked when she reached the porch.

"Sure that would be nice," Juliana replied, and snuggled into the rocking chair next to the one Michael had vacated. Michael disappeared into the house for a moment. He came back carrying a coffee and his Mom's old afghan. Juliana welcomed the warmth of the coffee and settled the multicolored, woolen afghan around her legs. "Thanks Michael, this is so cozzy."

"How are you feeling now? Will you be well enough to go back to work tomorrow?" she asked leaning closer and medically assessing what she saw.

"Yes I'm going back tomorrow. Still a little sore, but I'm ok."

It occurred to Juliana as they sat quietly sipping coffee and watching the stars come out, Michael would not be pleased with her news.

It gripped her heart, because she felt so at peace out here on this porch sitting with Michael. He may have come into hard times in his life, but he was still very dear to her, she realized. As she gently rocked in companionable silence it occurred to her that they made a wonderful couple. She could feel her face redden. She had never thought of Michael in that way before. She was grateful when Michael broke the silence.

"How is your Dad doing?"

"Oh, he'll be fine. But Dad's a terrible patient. He keeps my Mom busy waiting on him," she smiled.

Michael rose and taking both cups went in to freshen up their coffees. As she sat alone and waited for Michael to return, she thought of how handsome he looked tonight. His eyes were bluer and more intense than she remembered. He left in a boy's body and came back in a man's, muscular and tall. *What was she doing?* She could not continue with thoughts like this. As much as she liked Michael and cared for him, there could never be anything between them. It was impossible with the secret she held, she told herself.

Michael came back with two steaming cups of coffee. He smiled down at her as he handed her the pink mug.

"Are you warm enough?" he asked. "We can go in the house if you'd like," he offered.

"No, not unless you do, I'm fine." She pulled the afghan up further on to her shoulders and snuggled in.

Then Juliana brought up the subject of Jimmy and the wallet. She let Michael know Jimmy had discussed the incident with her. She knew Jimmy well enough to know someone placed the wallet in Jimmy's locker. When she proclaimed Jimmy innocent Michael felt relief that Jimmy hadn't changed.

As both chairs rocked in the same rhythm they watched fireflies flitting over the stubble in the hay field. Both lost in their own thoughts they heard an owl hoot from a distance behind the house. Juliana closed her eyes for just a second and enjoyed the peaceful evening. A deep longing came over her and she got up unexpectedly and gave Michael her mug.

"I'd better get home now," she said standing stiff and erect, "You have a good day back at work tomorrow." With that she was gone.

Michael wondered what had happened to make her want to leave so suddenly. He enjoyed her company. When she closed her eyes in prayer, he realized that he neglected his prayer time. His faith seemed so fragile now. He decided when he went to his room later, he would see if his old Bible was still in his room.

***

Michael walked down stairs to a big problem Monday morning. When he entered the kitchen, his mother and Jimmy were in the midst of a big argument. Jimmy stood waving a note.

"Mom I need you to come to school. We have a meeting with the principal about the wallet found in my locker."

"I'm not going," Michael's Mom yelled digging in her heels.

"Mom, I'm to bring you with me," Jimmy exclaimed louder and more frantic.

It was clear to Michael that his hung over Mother was in no shape see the principal.

"Can I make a suggestion," he broke into the argument.

"What," they both yelled together.

"I'll go with Jimmy." Jimmy looked at him as if he had grown two horns on his head but his mom was all for the idea.

Michael took Jimmy aside, "Jimmy come on, she's in no shape to go to the school."

Jimmy stood pondering this for a moment and then said, "Yeah."

The argument ended and Janet went back to bed. Michael talked to Scott to tell him he would be late for work and would drive himself out to the site after his appointment.

★★★

Michael and Jimmy sat and waited on a bench just outside the principal's office.

Jimmy sat and twirled his ball cap in his hands. Michael sat and gripped the seat and tapped his foot repeatedly.

Michael had a nightmare flashback to a similar bench that sat just outside a packed courtroom a little over five years ago. It took him back to the day they falsely accused him of robbing a store; the real thief must have put the loot in through the open window of Michael's car. The thief probably had plans to come back later and retrieve it. But meanwhile the police had found it during a spot check, and Michael looked extremely guilty.

He remembered fishing alone that day at the creek and leaving the car out at the roadway, while he had walked along the bank to his favorite fishing spot. Later that afternoon in town, the police asked if they could check his car. It totally shocked him when they pulled the parcel of money out from behind his front seat. With no plausible alibi, the police became convinced he lied. Caught with the money in his car the jury found him guilty.

After he spoke with Juliana and questioned Jimmy again on the way into town in the car, he felt they accused Jimmy wrongly as well.

Michael twisted his baseball cap in his hands as Mr. Brownlee, the school principal, came out of his office and shook a parent's hand. A little guy in about grade one stood looking thoroughly chastised. He peeked at Michael from behind his mother's skirt. Michael put a hand out and stopped Jimmy from twirling his pen through his fingers like a baton.

The principal turned his attention to him, and he shot to his feet and introduced himself. Jimmy slowly stood beside him.

"I'm Michael Ardath, Jimmy's brother. I'm sorry our Mother can't come today."

Mr. Brownlee motioned them into his office. Michael became aware that Mr. Brownlee knew of his past in prison and wanted to paint Jimmy with the same brush. Often during the conversation, he made disparaging uncalled-for remarks. Michael's temper boiled over when Mr. Brownlee stood up and said, "I have no choice but to take this to the police."

Is this the way people would treat him forever, he wondered. The injustice he endured; would it be Jimmy's fate too?

Michael grabbed Jimmy's arm when Jimmy angrily tried to get to his feet. Michael held tight to Jim's arm as they both got up and left the office.

On the way home Michael railed against the injustice. Then quietly Jimmy spoke from the passenger seat. "We need to pray Michael." Taken aback for a moment Michael gaped. Then Jimmy quoted 2 Corinthians 4:8 *"We are hard-pressed on every side, but not crushed; perplexed, but not in despair; persecuted, but not abandoned; struck down, but not destroyed."* "God will see me through this Michael. Remember Grandma Ardath used to always say 'this was sent to test you'. Well if this is a test I plan on passing it." Jimmy concluded.

Michael pondered Jimmy's words as they drove the rest of the way home. Had the last five years of his life been a big test and if so had he passed it?

Michael let Jimmy out at the road and drove on to the construction site further down the highway.

***

Jimmy crossed the highway and went to find Juliana. He found her in the horse barn. The minute Juliana heard him come in she stopped brushing Lightning and stepped out of the stall to ask why he was there in the middle of the morning. Jimmy ran right up to her and started to tell her about the trip to the principal's office. His eyes pleaded with her to understand.

"He actually thinks I took that dumb wallet," he told her, "He just wouldn't listen to Michael and me. They found it hidden in my locker, so I must have taken it. He says he will take the whole story to the police."

"Oh Jimmy," Juliana said putting her hand on his shoulder.

"This is just like Michael's trial," said Jimmy, tears very close to the surface.

"Have you talked to Lenny about this?" Juliana asked.

"No, I haven't had a chance to yet." He explained.

"Maybe Lenny can help you figure out who could have put the wallet in your locker," she advised. "Jimmy we will have to pray really hard about this. Only God can make this right."

***

Juliana left Jimmy in the barn. When she passed by living room her Mom and Dad were watching a movie, so she grabbed a coffee and went to the solarium. As she sat enjoying the solitude she began to think. It had taken courage for Michael to face Mr. Brownlee with Jimmy. She could see how that whole experience would have felt like going through his trial all over again. Something her grandfather had told her once came to mind, courage isn't <u>not </u>being afraid courage is being afraid and facing the fight in spite of the fear. And that was her Michael, he had been twenty years old and had gone into that courtroom every day five years ago and faced his accusers head on. He had gone against insurmountable odds and probably knew he would lose. But rather than run, he stood his ground and gave it his best shot. She just hoped that Jimmy would not have to face the same fate as Michael. She sat and prayed just as hard as she knew how that somehow God would come through for Jimmy.

CHAPTER EIGHT

Juliana loved apple picking season. So it was with great delight that she looked out her window to see a dozen cars and trucks parked along the Ardath's driveway. She watched as Hispanic men and older boys set up tents of various sizes and colors. Some looked like old army surplus tents faded and tattered around the edges. She smiled as kids helped their mothers by carrying their belongings into the tents. Juliana couldn't wait to participate in the apple picking.

She thought of how the air felt crisp and clear at this time of year, and it hardly ever rained. The nights were usually star lit, and the days were bright and warm with the sun shining down on her fall coat. She loved the special camaraderie in the orchard, while they picked the ripe apples everyone was happy and jovial. She loved hearing the night birds calling from nearby trees. When winter gathering became delayed, squirrels would protest loudly, like angry mothers who scolded their children. Mice scurried through the leaves on the ground, eager to reach the safety of their underground burrows among the roots of the trees. She thought of how rewarding it felt to go home at day's end with sore protesting muscles, and a sense that she had been a big help and had accomplished a great deal. A warm relaxing bath to sooth those sore muscles and a good night sleep. Then, she was ready to go back again.

When Juliana was younger she had to wait until after supper, then with dishes done and homework complete, she could go to help.

Her mother didn't like her "mixing with those children", so Juliana often didn't let on to her mother where she went. As far as her parents knew, she had gone off to play outside. As a child, she helped sort and wash the apples with the older women and children. As a teen they allowed her to pick or carry full baskets to the sorters. Now as an adult, she could climb a ladder and pick the apples. There was a special feeling up high off the ground where the tree branches surrounded her. She felt an amazing sense of accomplishment as basket after basket became filled.

Juliana kept watch off and on all-day as the apple pickers settled in. After supper she noticed activity in the front of Ardath's yard had stopped. That could mean only one thing; everyone was out behind the house picking apples in the orchard. Juliana finished her Mom's dishes, checked the thermometer at the back door and dressed appropriately then went across the road to help pick apples.

She recognized Carlos right away; he was the man in charge. She walked up to him and offered her help. Carlos recognized her from past years. His one arm around her shoulders felt good as he showed her his crude map of the orchard. He pointed to the row where he wanted her to work, and told her where to find a ladder. He gave her one final squeeze of her shoulders and sent her off to find her row.

As she walked through the orchard with her heavy ladder, many of the pickers recognized her and either called out or waved. She recognized many of the children she had grown up playing hide-and-seek with. They were now adults with small children of their own. They waved and called out as she walked by the weight of the ladder biting into her shoulder. She looked forward to break time when she could meet all of them once again and catch up on what had happened in their lives.

She found the row of trees assigned to her and set up her ladder. Awkward and heavy, it took a moment to get it positioned. She felt delighted to find that Jimmy would be her runner. He would supply her with baskets and take the full ones back to the women to sort and wash the apples. She gave him a smile full of fondness as he handed her a harness and her first basket. He helped her clip her harness and get her basket positioned in it, and then she climbed up the ladder and started to pick ripe apples.

This was all just as she remembered it. Stars began to peek out between the twisted branches of the tree. She had disturbed a squirrel in her tree, and he had retreated to the end of a branch and hung on for dear life as the branch swayed under his weight. She smiled as he chattered and scolded her for invading his space. She quickly got busy and plucked ripe apples the way Carlos had taught her. She twisted them in such a way the stem came off with the apple leaving the tree undamaged.

It took her a while to get back in the familiar rhythm. Soon her basket became full, and she climbed down to hand it to Jimmy. She repositioned her ladder and went back up with a new basket. It was pleasant up here above the rest of the world surrounded by this old tree's branches. She could let her thoughts wander. Wander to Michael and the last time she had seen him. While trapped in that landslide of dirt Michael frightened her. Oh, what if he had died that day. Her chest filled with pain and tightness like a heart attack victim at the thought of it. It suddenly occurred to her, that life would have a large hole in it if Michael were gone. Sadness swept over her at the thought, and she thanked God that Michael hadn't died that day.

While lost in her thoughts, the darkness thickened. When she took her next basket down to Jimmy, he announced that Carlos had decided they would quit for the night. She grabbed one side of the basket, and together they carried it back to the sorting tables. Mrs. Ardath gave hot chocolate to everyone. Juliana took a cup and talked with all of her old friends. Hector stood nearby. He was one of her hide-and-seek playmates. Michael walked up and they reminisced about things they had gotten into when they were kids. Soon Hector's wife Maria came out of their tent carrying their baby. She showed him off to them and Juliana asked if she could hold him. Maria had him securely wrapped in a warm soft blanket; all that peeked out was his little round face and a shock of black hair.

Something warm and liquid happened in Juliana's heart as she looked down at the bundle in her sore tired arms. Michael's face was suddenly close as he cooed at the wee babe. She looked up at Michael's face and saw the huge measure of love he shone down on the little guy. He will make an amazing father someday, she thought. She had no doubt in her mind about that fact. From the light that shone from his eyes she could tell he would have much love to give a little boy.

More of the apple pickers came up to them then, and someone suggested they play a game of hide-and-seek for old time sake. Juliana handed the baby back to his mother and looked to Michael to see what he would say. "Sure why not," he responded. Maria and the baby joined the people gathered around a bond fire started in the side yard to keep everyone warm.

They declared Hector "it" and the rest of the group laughed and gleefully scattered to find a hiding place. Jimmy was a part of the group. The teen grabbed Juliana's hand and dragged her with him into the trees at the south end of the house. Michael soon joined them. Michael stood behind a tree while Jimmy and Juliana crouched in the tall grass. They whispered and giggled among themselves until Hector headed their way. Jimmy panicked and took off in a crouch toward the safety of the back of the barn. Hector had stopped momentarily and checked some shrubbery at the side of the house. Any minute, he would turn his attention to the stand of oak trees where Michael and Juliana hid. Suddenly Michael ran over grabbed Juliana's hand and dragged her to her feet. They followed the line of trees out to the ditch by the road in front of the house. They lay in the ditch that they had hid in many years before. They watched and chuckled as Hector went right to the line of old trees where they had just left. Juliana giggled uncontrollably. She tried not to make any noise. She rolled on to her back and held her ribs with both arms. She watched Michael's face as he propped himself up on his elbows beside her in the grassy ditch. He lay on his stomach. Just his head peeked over the edge like a turtle looked out of his shell. He watched to see if Hector would come their way. As in the past, they were safe in the ditch. Hector turned and headed in the opposite direction. Michael visibly relaxed, and their eyes met. Slowly Michael's expression changed from laughter to something more serious. Juliana searched his face and tried to read his thoughts. He had become very quiet; he looked intently into her eyes. Then just as naturally as if he had done it many times, he leaned down and kissed her. Her arms came up to either side of his waist at first as if to pushed him away, her fight or flight response, and then as if to hold him in place. The kiss was short as kisses go but so sweet. It had left both of them shaken. Michael had lifted his head slightly but his face was still just inches from hers. Now he visibly explored her face for her reaction. She looked up at him with round startled eyes.

"What just happened?" Juliana asked, in a soft hushed voice.

"Gee I don't know," Michael said, a mystified tone to his voice.

The warmest feeling had spread through Juliana. Something she had never experienced before. It frightened her a little. This can't happen, she told herself. Not now, it's too late now.

Michael shifted his weight away from her then and rolled over on to his back. Both lay quietly and processed what had just happened. All the stars had come out now. Light from thousands of years ago shone down on two bran knew lovers.

CHAPTER NINE

Juliana snuggled into bed that night still in shock over what had occurred in a grassy ditch a few yards away. After she said prayers and waited for sleep to come, she felt that warm, happy, contented feeling again. She realized that Michael was at the center of that feeling. Is this what love is like, she asked herself. If this is it, no wonder people all over the world go in search to find it. She hadn't searched for it, but it had found her on a cold fall night in a leaf filled ditch. She wondered what Michael must think. He looked as awe struck as she felt. Someone had called from the front porch the game was over. Michael came to his senses first and offered her a hand up. She had stood and looked up into his face, all shadowy in the dark.

"I best go home now," she had whispered. Michael nodded. When she reached the opposite side of the highway, she looked back. Michael still stood in the same spot. He waved, and she went on. She eventually drifted off to sleep thinking of all the times she and Michael had done sweet loving acts for each other during their childhood.

***

When Michael went to bed that night, he put on his pajamas, and finished in the bathroom then got down on his knees beside his bed. He had not knelt to pray like this since he was a boy. But tonight he wanted God to know that he meant business. He folded his hands in prayer just as he had as a child, closed his eyes tightly and prayed.

"Heavenly Father, first I want to thank you for bringing me safely through the landside. I thank you that Juliana brought me comfort and strength. I pray Lord, that you will be with Jimmy to help him solve the mystery of the wallet. And please Lord speak to my mom about her drinking. And finally Lord, I want to talk to you about what happened with Juliana tonight. I like her a lot Lord. And I know I don't stand a chance with her. First,

I'll never be wealthy like her dad. And second, because of what happened five years ago, my wrongful conviction, I will always have a cloud hanging over my life." Michael paused then and tried to decide how to go on. "I guess what I want to say Lord, is that I would love to spend the rest of my life with Juliana. She is the one that could make all of my dreams come true. I will leave this with you Lord, like Grandma Ardath taught me to do. Amen."

The following Sunday Michael got up and dressed for church. His muscles were still a little sore, from all the apple picking he had done all week after work. He used muscles he didn't usually use. It delighted Jimmy last night, when Michael had let him know that he wanted to go to church with him. They had tried to talk Mom into coming too, but she had declined.

Juliana gave them both a sweet welcoming smile, when they slipped into the pew beside her. It felt good to share a hymnbook and stand beside her and sing. Something had definitely changed between them. They had camaraderie, and "a sweet knowing" that had not been there before. They kept stealing glances at each other.

After church Jimmy asked if they could go to the café for coffee. He had big news for them. Juliana said she could and followed them over in her car.
After the server delivered coffee to their booth, Jimmy began his explanation of the wallet mystery.

Juliana grabbed Michael's hand under the table as they listened intently.
"You will never believe this," Jimmy started. "I finally got a chance to go over to Lenny's last night. I told him about the

police involvement, and how I need to know who put the wallet in my locker.

He could tell I was distraught and mystified about how it had gotten into my locker."

"Did he have any ideas?" asked Michael.

"I'm getting to that," said Jimmy, with a teen's typical impatience.

Michael and Juliana exchanged looks.

Jimmy took another sip of his milk loaded coffee and went on. "He knew exactly who took it," Jimmy said, building up the suspense.

"Well who?" Juliana wanted to know.

"He did," said Jimmy, with a strange grin on his face.

"What," Michael exploded.

Several people turned to see what the loud exclamation was all about. Michael held up a hand to let the people know everything was all right, and to go back to their meal.

The three exchanged a conspirator's grin, and Jimmy went on. "Yes, it was Lenny"

"How can that be? He's your best friend isn't he?" asked Michael.

"Yes he is. But here's the thing. He explained that since I am a Christian, and I live my life as I should, he was jealous. He knew I live my life the way he should live his life. I guess it bugged him, so he took Hal's wallet and planted it in my locker. I guess he tried to bring me down a peg or two."

Michael and Juliana exchanged a glance and shook their heads.

"Thank goodness, Lenny and I are good friends, and his conscience got to him."

"Boy, you're right there Jim, it could have turned out differently," said Juliana.

"Yea," said Michael "I had visions of my ordeal all over again."

"Well, later this afternoon Lenny's parents will drive us into the police station to explain it all to the police."

"Well, maybe if Hal doesn't press charges it will all blow over," said Michael.

"It sounds like Lenny learned a valuable lesson," stated Juliana.

"Yea, he says he will start to come out to youth group," Jimmy told them, proudly.

They finished their coffee, and Jimmy waited in the car as Michael said good-bye to Juliana. They wished each other a good week, and then Michael watched as Juliana pulled out of the parking space.

Later that afternoon Michael offered to go with Jimmy to the police station. But Jimmy said he would be fine because Lenny's dad would be there. Michael worried all afternoon while they were gone. He had flashbacks to the way the police treated him when his incident happened. He thought he should have insisted on going, because the not knowing made him crazy. His imagination ran rampant.

It was a relief when Jimmy finally came through the door and said that they accepted Lenny's confession. He had no idea what would happen if it went to court, but they knew now that Jimmy had nothing to do with the stolen wallet. Michael felt so relieved that God had answered his prayer. God spared Jimmy that horrible ordeal.

Later that night, they had a problem with Michael's mother, Janet. She worried about Jimmy's trip to the police station too. Instead of handling it by pacing and praying as Michael had done, she had sat in her room and drank all-day. Then by evening she had come out to have supper with the boys and fell and split her head open. It bled profusely, so while Michael got a towel to get the blood stopped, Jimmy called over to Juliana's.

As soon as Juliana received the message that Janet cut her head, she went right over. When she arrived at the Ardath's door, Janet sat in a chair in the kitchen. Michael had the towel tightly wrapped to slow the bleeding. He had Jimmy press an ice pack to the area of the wound through the towel. Janet seemed disoriented. Now, not only was she drunk, she had a nasty gash on her head. Michael watched as Juliana convinced her to let her take a look at the open wound. Mrs. Ardath didn't even know who Juliana was at first and put up a fight. Finally, she came out of her stupor and recognized Juliana. When Juliana finally had a look at the wound, she said she definitely needed stitches. It took them a few minutes to convince Janet that she needed to go to the hospital. By this time, she had sobered up enough to realize what a bad state she was in, and she begun to cry. Juliana worked miracles with her. She sat in the backseat of the car with her and talked to her all the way to the hospital. Juliana had dealt with alcoholics as part of her training and seemed to know just what to say.

They admitted Janet to the ER and sat quietly and waited to talk to the doctor. Juliana called home to let her parents know what had happened. Michael listened as she reassured them that Michael would bring her home later.

Dr. Bennett came out after a while to talk to them. He took them to a quiet room to have a serious talk with the Ardath boys. Dr. Bennett had been the town doctor for years and knew all of them well. He explained that he had stitched up Janet's head and sat her down for a serious talk about her drinking. He explained that he approached the subject with her many times before. But this time, he sensed that she wanted to make a change. He didn't know if it was all the blood or the bang on the head, but she wanted to stop the vicious cycle of drinking. He recommended he keep her there in the hospital a couple of days, until he could admit her to a bed in a rehab facility. He wanted to make sure Michael and Jimmy could manage while she was gone. Michael reassured Dr. Bennett that he would take responsibility for Jimmy, while their mother took care of her problem.

He allowed the boys to see their mother. She appeared bruised and pale with a large bandage on her head. She gave them a sheepish look, when they entered the room. Jimmy ran to the hospital bed and gave her a hug over the rails of the bed. Michael stood back and watched fighting back tears. He hoped that his mother was serious, and she would be able to stay sober afterwards.

When his turn came, Michael hugged his Mom tightly and whispered in her ear. "Do the work mom."

She gave him a reassuring smile through her tears and whispered back, "I will son."

Michael knew through his experience with prison AA that she would have to work through and follow the twelve step AA program. It would be one of the hardest tasks his Mom would ever face. He knew, because his cell mate had gone through it.

They both said good-bye to their Mom and promised to come back after supper the following night to visit.

They went back to Juliana in the lounge, where she patiently waited. They decided to go back to Ardath's for hot chocolate, before they took Juliana home. It amazed Michael when they got back to the house; Juliana just dug right in and helped Jimmy get the hot chocolate ready. It embarrassed Michael that Mom still hadn't kept the house tidy. Juliana didn't mind she just made her self at home and helped Jimmy find what he needed.

As they sipped hot chocolate and talked, Juliana thought of how hard this must be for Jimmy at seventeen to have his Mother sent away for a least a month. She determined that she would be sure to check in on "the boys" regularly and offer any assistance that she could. Juliana helped tidy the kitchen. They finished, and Michael walked her home.

"Thanks for being so good with my Mom," Michael said, as they walked along.

"No problem Michael," she said, giving his hand a squeeze. "Jimmy can always give me a call when you aren't around," she reassured him.

"Thanks, I appreciate that," he told her.

Things started to change between them; their lives had begun to intertwine slowly. Neither of them had realized it yet.

When they got to Juliana's door they stood for a moment uncertain. Both remembered the kiss from the other night and neither knew how to proceed. Michael could tell by the way they both hesitated. They were playmates all of their lives. These newfound feelings felt strange and frightened them. They were both uncertain and didn't want to do something to change the wondrous thing that began to happen between them. In the end they gave each other a long hug. Michael's eyes glistened with tears, as he said goodnight and turned to go.

CHAPTER TEN

Juliana awoke the next morning to the sound of birds on the roof. It was dawn. Light just began to infuse the world. Juliana peeked out long enough to get a sense of the time and rolled over and snuggled in again. She lay quietly as her thoughts drifted down pleasant avenues when the thought suddenly came.

My news will ruin everything.

How could she have let herself ignore this? Juliana never once thought of the things that bothered Michael. Like the fact that she came from a higher station in life than he did. Or that he would never be able to keep her in the lifestyle that she had lived in until now. No, she worried about Michael's reaction to her secret. Tears filled her eyes as the heartbreak rolled over her. Oh, to have finally found love and then have it taken away, if Michael couldn't handle her secret. She lay and cried. She let the tears stream down the side of her face into her pillow. She gave in to despair. When she had finally run out of tears, she pondered what to do. The secret needed telling, it would not remain a secret forever. It was best to have it out in the open, and then she could deal with it. She prayed that God would give her the strength to deal with everyone's reaction, and that God would show her how best to go on.

This problem had niggled at the back of her mind long enough. She had kept her thoughts private too long. She got up, dressed and went to find her Mom and Dad to tell her Dad the news and face the consequences.

She found them both in the solarium. They had finished their breakfast and sat drinking coffee. Juliana sat down with a coffee and gave her Mom a look. She could tell her Mom knew right away what Juliana intended to do. She pulled her chair in, cradled her coffee on the table between her hands and tried to steady her nerves.

"Dad, I need to talk to you," she started. "I have something to tell you, that you are not going to like." There, she had gotten this far, now to turn back was not an option. Her Dad gave her a quizzical look and waited for her to go on. "About six months ago, I did a very foolish thing."

Her dad's eyes widened, but she pressed on. "I met a soldier from the army base a few miles from the nursing school residence. His name is Jared. We dated off and on, Mom probably mentioned him." Her parents exchanged a glance. Juliana could tell her dad wondered what she tried to lead up to, so she pressed ahead. "We started becoming close, and one night he took me to a party that one of his friends threw off the base." Her knuckles had become white, as she grasped the table. "They served punch, and I guess there was vodka in it, because I didn't know they spiked it. Afterwards, I realized I should have known soldiers didn't just serve fruit punch." Juliana paused to catch her breath; it felt like all the life had sucked out of her. This felt like the most difficult conversation she had ever had. "Anyway to make a long story short, I slept with Jared that night." She tried desperately to hold the tears back that burned in the back of her throat and wanted to spill from her eyes. Her mother had grabbed her father's hand, as he stirred in his chair. "Daddy, I felt so bad afterward but it was too late." Tears escaped; she couldn't hold them back now. Juliana's dad sat with his arms crossed and waited for her to finish. "I'm so sorry Daddy, I'm pregnant." She blurted, and then completely gave in to the tears. She sobbed uncontrollably, and her Mom rushed over to hug her. Her parents exchanged a look across the table.

There was anger clear in her dad's voice. "Where is this young man now?"

Juliana's sobs deepened so Juliana's Mom said. "They've broken up, Harvey."

"What," he exclaimed," you knew about this."

"Not for long dear," Marion tried to explain. She sent him a look begging him to understand.

"Well what is this young man prepared to do about this?" he wanted to know.

"He wants nothing to do with it. He has shipped out and told me to lose his number." Juliana tried to explain through her tears.

"Well that's just great," her dad said, as he got up and stomped out of the room.

Juliana's mom patted her on the back and tried to calm her down and console her.

"What now Mom?" Juliana finally asked, when the crying turned to small gasps.

"Give your Dad some time, sweetie. He needs time to process all of this, and then he will be ready for us to reason with him," her Mom advised her. They were both emotionally drained now. When Juliana got to her feet, her mother stood and hugged her for a long moment. "Don't forget God is still with you," her mother said, as she left the room to go and see where Harvey had gone.

Juliana did what she always did when she felt forlorn and needed comfort. She got her coat on and went out to the horse barn to see Lightning. He waited as always with a friendly welcome, and a big warm shoulder to cry on. As she brushed him and saddled him she started to feel a little better. She didn't want to meet anyone on her ride, so she took him out through one of the pastures, and onto a path that led through the woods north of the house.

She rode deep into the forest and stopped. The trees were extremely tall here and bare of branches at the bottom. They towered high above her. The sun dappled the forest floor with the little bit of sunlight that could penetrate the canapé of leaves and needles above. Everything became hushed here, nothing stirred. Juliana always felt as if she had come into a cathedral when she came here. God definitely dwelled here. She sat quietly on Lightning's back and felt all the emotions her pregnancy brought to her, sadness and shame, because of the baby's conception. Hurt and fear, because of the way her father had reacted. Ashamed and forlorn, because of the way people would feel about the baby. But elated and excited, because a tiny, sweet, innocent baby grew inside her. She let the emotions wash over her; she experienced one after the other. At times she felt it wasn't her fault, and she felt at times they duped her with the spiked punch. Then she would feel that it was her fault. In her sober mind she knew how wrong she had been to sleep with Jared. Then she felt anger because if she stayed sober she never would have gone that far.

Then Michael came into her mind, and the tears that she had been able to hold back spilled down her cheeks. She had been in a fog the last few days. She had allowed

herself to reignite feelings that probably lay dormant since childhood. She loved Michael, she knew she did. She suspected that he had feelings for her too. How could she ever tell him about the baby? It would break his heart and that was the last thing she wanted to do. It would hurt him, and she couldn't avoid it. He would never want her after she told him. She hadn't brought anything to wipe her tears with. Lightning's neck and her jeans were wet with her tears. The wind had picked up. It came time to head back. She said a weak, silent prayer and turned to go home. She turned and something moved to her right. A small baby deer stood nearby. It had lifted its head and stood perfectly still and stared at her with its big round brown eyes. Neither of them moved. Lightning didn't either. A strange feeling came over her. Something stirred in the leaves and the fawn darted away. The spell broke. Juliana felt peace and reassurance. She gave Lightning his head and they went home.
***

    Michael worked to fix the sadly leaning back door. As he worked he thought about his life. He felt glad that they cleared Jimmy of the wallet incident. He was proud of the way Jimmy handled it. He leaned on scripture and believed that God would come through for him. He was ecstatic that his Mom would finally go to rehab. He worried that perhaps she wouldn't stay though. That could always happen. He had a good job that he enjoyed. He felt like part of the crew now. He teased and fooled around with the rest of the guys. He realized that some of the thick skin and hardness that he developed in prison had begun to drop away now. He determined to rise above life's circumstances, and be a good person no matter how people treated him. He found his old bible right where he had left it. He began to read it for a short time at night after he got into bed. And then there was Juliana, wonderful, beautiful Juliana. Lately he had noticed a light in her eyes when she looked at him. It made him feel so fantastic inside. It made him feel like maybe, just maybe, he could have a happy future someday. He decided if he wanted Juliana in his future; he had to come up with a plan to revitalize the orchard. It was in neglect and needed proper pruning. He needed to buy spray for next spring and make sure the sprayer still worked properly. He needed to check all the equipment. The farm could support a family; he just needed to work hard and be patient. It wouldn't happen overnight, but maybe one day he could be worthy enough to ask Juliana to share his life. As he put the finishing touches on the sagging door, warmth and joy infused him.

***

A few days later Juliana sat having her morning coffee with her Mom in the solarium. Although her mother is unhappy about the baby's conception, it thrilled her to help plan for the baby's arrival. Juliana had an appointment scheduled with Dr. Bennett for the next week.

"I think we should go to Baby World in the city," suggested Marion, "it's only an hour away."

"If you don't mind me using your sewing machine, I would love to make some nightgowns for the baby. We could look at material at Fabric Junction."

"Oh, that's a good idea you can make receiving blankets too. And I can pick up yarn and make a shawl and a sweater outfit."

Juliana took another sip of her coffee and thought how wonderful it felt to have her mother on her side. Her dad was incredibly upset and disturbed, as an out of wedlock pregnancy would reflect negatively on his social status. Juliana realized now that bad things can happen to Christians too. But the more she read her Bible the more she felt it's not the circumstances we are in, but the way we handle the circumstances that concerns God. The Bible says "our motives are weighted" by the Lord. Juliana had decided that for the baby's sake; she would take the high road and do her best to give it a good upbringing.

"We'll get Manuel to look for your old cradle and crib. We stored them in the rafters of the old barn. We'll need a new mattress and sheets too," said Marion, as she became visibly enthusiastic.

They finished their coffee. Marion made sure Harvey was all right alone for a few hours while they went to the city to shop. Juliana made sandwiches and left them for his lunch in case they weren't back until late afternoon.

CHAPTER ELEVEN

Michael spoke to Jimmy about his plans to refurbish the apple orchard. Consulted about the plans to get the neglected orchard back into shape, Jimmy became excited.

"What does all this involve?"

"A lot of hard work," said Michael, with a glint in his eye. "The good news is dad has left behind the equipment we need. I've taken a look and most of it is in good shape."

"I can help pay for new stuff with the money I get from working at Winslow's," Jimmy said, showing an enthusiasm Michael had not expected.

"What kind of stuff do we need?" asked Jimmy.

"Well a cherry picker would be useful," said Michael teasing Jimmy. A cherry picker was a hydraulic piece of huge equipment that would cost up to $3,000 dollars used.

"Oh yea I'll just get right on that," said Jimmy, with a typical teen reply.

"You wouldn't happen to know where dad's old books are on how to prune and care for the trees?"

"Yea, I think I do."

"I remember something about different methods depending on how old the trees are.

You don't trim a four-year old tree the same way as a one-year old."

"Why prune them anyway?" asked Jimmy.

"We have to trim them to get the most fruit to grow. If you leave too many leaves, the tree will be busy growing them instead of our moneymaking apples," explained Michael.

"Sounds like we have a lot to learn, Bro," said Jimmy.

"Yes, well it will be worth it in the end," said Michael, thinking of a long blond haired young woman, he had recently kissed in a ditch.

It turned out the boys had trouble finding their dad's old apple care books. The next time they visited their Mother, they would ask her where to find them. Luckily they caught her the day before she left the hospital to go into the rehab facility.

It was a teary good-bye but both men were happy that their mother would get the help she needed. The doctor reassured them the worse part was over, the physical detoxification of the alcoholic's body. Now they would work on "the cure", the mental part of the illness. They would delve into why she abused the alcohol. Michael reminded him it had started after their Dad had passed away.

***

Juliana had already faced the worst day of her young life. Now she faced another. She needed to tell Michael about the baby. In Juliana's mind a lot rode on Michael's reaction to her news.

If he could not accept another man's baby, her friendship and their future together would end. Juliana knew that Michael was a good person and would face the criticism of others to be with him. In her mind everything depended on Michael. Did he care enough for her? To be fair to him, she needed to tell him right away. If he didn't love her, it would be easier to walk away now. If she had been selfish, she could have kept her secret and continued the romantic relationship until she had him hooked. He would have found it harder to walk away later. But Juliana just couldn't do that. She loved him too much to deceive him like that. His happiness was more important to her than her own.

It was with all of this in mind that she called Michael and asked if she could come and pick him up in her car after supper one night.

Michael came out of his house with a big smile on his face; obviously he looked forward to spend time with Juliana. He hugged her and kissed her cheek, he didn't suspect a thing. She would blindside him, and he didn't have a clue.

Juliana didn't drive far. She came to a driveway into one of her dad's fields and pulled into it off the highway. Juliana slipped the car into park and turned to face Michael.

"We need to talk," Juliana said, the smile on Michael's face faded by degrees, as he registered the serious expression on her face.

"What is it Jewels?" he asked, and used a name he hadn't used since they were teens.

"You're not making this easy," Juliana told him, pulling both of her hands from the grip he had taken on them.

"You know I've been fond of you since we were kids," she started, "and it's because of that, I want to be the one to tell you a secret I've kept. I want you to hear it from me."

"Juliana it's ok," he tried to reassure her.

Juliana swallowed hard and plunged on. "While I attended nursing school I met a guy named Jared. We dated for quite awhile. He was a soldier from Camp Harper."

Michael sat quietly listening, a concerned expression on his face.

"We went to a party one night and they spiked the punch." Tears stung her eyes now.

Michael grabbed her hand. She didn't pull away this time, she went on instead.

"I ended up sleeping with him that night," she stated simply.

"That's in the past," Michael said, trying to defuse the impact of her words.

The tears spilled down her face then.

"I'm pregnant."

Michael's eyes widened as the shock hit him.

Juliana tried to wipe the tears away. She wanted to clear her eyes, so she could gage Michael's reaction.

Michael's grip had loosened on Juliana's hand.

When she cleared her eyes enough to get an impression of how Michael felt about this, she couldn't tell. Seconds ticked by.

"Are you ok Jewels?" he asked, clearing his throat.

He was putting his own feelings aside to find out how she coped, she assumed.

"With all of this I mean."

"Yes, I'm ok, yes I am."

"When is the baby due?" he wanted to know.

Juliana was incredulous. Instead of being upset or disappointed Michael wanted to know if she and the baby were all right.

"I'm six and a half months now," she told him. I can't keep the secret much longer," she confessed. "People will start to notice. I think some are suspicious all ready."

"Well, we'll just have to face them and their curiosity won't we," said Michael squeezing her hand.

Juliana couldn't believe what he said. It sounded like Michael was ok with the baby.

"I will understand if you want to walk away," said Juliana trying to give him an out.

"I won't be going anywhere."

Juliana started to sob in earnest then, and Michael wrapped reassuring arms around her.

Juliana went home from their meeting in a fog. Could this really be true? Could Michael accept a child that wasn't his own? Could they raise the child together and become a happy family? Would Michael change his mind after he had time to think about all of this? Only time would tell so once again Juliana decided to leave it with the Lord.

★★★

Harvey and Marion sat in the solarium early one morning about a month later. They sat enjoying the beautiful fall morning just before Thanksgiving. They had discussed their plans for the Thanksgiving celebration a couple of days before with Juliana. Juliana had mentioned that she would like to have Michael come and have Thanksgiving dinner with them. Both Harvey and Marion had been aware that Juliana and

Michael had seen a lot of each other in the last month. But neither of them wanted Michael to join the family for Thanksgiving. They came up with a plan to take Juliana away somewhere for Thanksgiving, and that way they would not have to explain why they didn't want Michael with them.

It was for this reason, Juliana found herself bored to tears at her Aunt Josephine's house. She had looked forward to spending Thanksgiving with Michael and his brother Jimmy, but her parents had given her no choice and off to Aunt Josephine's they went. Her one saving grace was that Aunt Joe had a dog named Sparky. How Sparky had that name was a total mystery to Juliana. Sparky was a small white "fur ball" of a dog. If he ever had any spark in him, it had long since left. He was old and moved rather slow. According to Juliana's dad his sister Joe had mollycoddled the dog and made a lap pet out of it. It was just these rather negative character traits that endeared the little dog to Juliana. She joyfully offered to take Sparky for a walk. It got her out of the house, and as she walked her Aunt Joe's dog around the small town neighborhood it gave her time to think. She thought about her baby, and what it would look like. Would it come with her flowing blond hair and brown eyes? Would its nose turn up ever so slightly at the end? Or would it have Jared's curly black hair and midnight brown eyes. As she and Sparky made the rounds of the neighborhood, Sparky left his scent on what seemed like every tree and fire hydrant. Juliana wondered some more about if the baby was a boy or girl. Would it be a fussy baby or a good baby?

She hoped it would be healthy and happy. She had started to read books on how to parent. Now that she knew her Mom and Dad would let her stay with them, she could embrace the thought of keeping the baby and try to become the best possible parent. Now she hoped the days would rush by until the baby's birth.

Thanksgiving was a somber affair with her Mom, Dad and Aunt Joe. It had been boring for twenty old Juliana. So when she gave Aunt Joe and Sparky one final hug each, she felt glad to head back home and the prospect of spending time with Michael.

CHAPTER TWELVE

Michael spent Thanksgiving missing Juliana. He went though the motions for Jimmy's sake. He purchased a good-sized turkey. They both worked on the meal together. They stuffed the turkey and peeled the potatoes. Michael had bought the trimmings cranberries, turnip and a medley of vegetables to steam. They would even have a store-bought pumpkin pie for dessert. The activity helped some, but by mid-afternoon he felt bad. Juliana's parents whisked her off to parts unknown to see an Aunt that he had never even heard Juliana mention before. She was some elderly maiden aunt that lived alone with her dog. He felt empty and sad without Juliana.

He expected his Mom home for the Thanksgiving meal at supper time. Granted a day out of the rehab, his Mother and a friend she had met there would come home for the meal. He and Jimmy watched TV and played video games until Mom and her guest arrived.

It felt so good to see their mother, she looked so much better. She came in and introduced her new friend, Barry. He reminded the boys of Andy Griffith. He was a big friendly man with a ready smile and a kind manner. They all enjoyed the meal the boys had prepared and had a pleasant evening with a now sober Mother. Barry even helped do dishes with Michael while Jimmy showed his mom what he had worked on in school. It felt good to have the old mom back. Jimmy told his mom about Juliana and she wanted to go see her. She expressed disappointment to find out that she was away.

"I'll have to write to her then," Janet decided.

"Thanks Mom," said Jimmy, "she could use support right now. Her dad isn't happy with her."

"I imagine the old biddies in town have a lot to say too."

"She hasn't mentioned it to me, but yea I bet they have." Jimmy agreed.

"You know son I have always taught you not to be judgmental. We have no idea what we might do under the same circumstances."

"I know Mom," Jimmy said, giving his Mom a one-arm hug. "Thanks."

Before they all knew it, the time had passed and it came time for Barry and Janet to get on the road and back to the rehab. It was a tearful good-bye and bittersweet as it was obvious to both boys a positive change had taken place in their Mother.

It got late and Jimmy had school the next day so he headed to bed. Michael took a few minutes to straighten the living room and prepare lunches for tomorrow.

Once again the loneliness hit him. He wished with all his heart he could see Juliana right then. Or even just talk to her on the phone would have helped.

When had he become so attached to her? She was the center of his universe suddenly. It seemed like very little else mattered. Juliana. Juliana. Juliana. He had sure changed a lot since he had come home from prison. His whole perspective on life had softened forty five degrees. His relationship with God was better and he felt that was a big part of the change. He read his Bible every night before he turned out the lights. That had made a big difference. Having Juliana care about him had made a huge difference too. With his plans to refurbish the orchard and make it a moneymaker again had been a big boon to his confidence and self-esteem. With Juliana at his side and God in their corner he felt he could face anything the world wanted to throw at the two of them. "Bring it on," he said as he turned out the kitchen light and climbed the stairs to where his Bible waited.

***

   The next few weeks passed in a blur for Juliana. She and her Mother made baby clothes. They had receiving blankets, nightgowns and burping pads made. Juliana's Mom had made two sweater outfits, one in yellow and one in green to bring the baby home in. One was a little bigger than the other, so Juliana could choose the one that fit the best. She planned to make more. It depended on what gender the baby turned out to be. Manuel the stable man got the crib and cradle out of storage. He invited Michael to help him refinish them. He brought them over to the Ardath's barn and they spent hours in the evenings working on them. They stripped and stained Juliana's old cradle in a mahogany stain. She and her mother then made padding and blankets to fit.
   Janet had surprised everyone when she had come home one weekend for a visit and had brought a wooden mobile that she and Barry had made in a crafting class. Barry had cut out little barnyard animals and Janet had painted them in great detail. It was one of a kind and really cute. Each animal had round, fat, little bodies, lovable. Juliana hugged Janet and wiped away tears. Janet had been true to her word and had written to Juliana, words of encouragement and support that Juliana needed.

***

   It happened on a Tuesday night, the pains started. Juliana had been with Michael earlier in the evening. She had walked over to his place after supper and showed him some baby clothes she had made. She felt restless and full of energy all-day. Michael came to the door and greeted her with a kiss.

"Hi, come on in."

Jimmy waved to her from the kitchen table, where he worked to finish his homework. Her hair had become wet in the rain. Michael took her coat and got her a towel to dry off her hair.

"We don't want you to catch cold," he said with a fond smile. "What have you got there?" he said. He noticed the bag she had brought with her. She showed him her handy work. "Wow, you are really good at this." He exclaimed with pride. "You will be able to go into business someday."

"Oh I'll soon have my hands full," she quipped, patting her swollen belly unconsciously.

"What have you been up to?"

Michael got out the plans he had worked on for the orchard. "I've projected the increase in productivity for the orchard next year. If I put all the plans into place, I will have doubled the yield of apples next year. Then with that money I plan to buy and plant more trees the following year." Michael told her.

"Oh Michael that's great," she said. She took the plans and had a look.

An unofficial understanding between them had formed. When Michael got on his feet financially, they would seriously consider marriage. They had become close and had spent time together in the last couple of months. Both of them had prayed long and hard and felt that God wanted them together.

Juliana still felt very restless. She had hot chocolate with "the boys" as she still called them, then Jimmy walked home with her. He went to work in the Winslow's barn and she went in to settle in for the night with a good book.

She awoke about two fifteen. At first she thought that her body had awoke because she needed to use the washroom. She lay on her side, all snuggled in warmly under her comforter. She didn't want to have to get out. She lay and savored the warm cuddly feeling and wished the urge to get up would go away. Then the first pain hit. It didn't last long and she thought maybe it was just the baby kicking around or perhaps it lay in the wrong spot. The second one hit a few minutes later as she got up and put on her dressing gown. The third one hit when she stood and washed her hands at the sink. By then she realized this wasn't the baby moving around. She panicked for a brief moment. The baby wasn't due for another month or more. She took a quick shower and reasoned the baby was far enough along to survive if born this early.

She timed the contractions now and they were sporadic but close together so she dressed and woke her Mother. She took her suitcase downstairs and waited while her Mom woke her dad and both of them dressed. She sat in the foyer on an embroidered antique chair and waited. Her dad rushed by on his way to get the car warmed up, his cane clunked on the foyer floor. Juliana felt scared but the worried and harried look on her dad's face made her smile. She thought of Michael then and wished with all of her heart that he had been this baby's father, and then he would be the one taking her to the hospital. He would be the one allowed to hold her hand and coach her through the rough time ahead. She made her Mother promise to call Michael the moment the baby came, and he was to be her first visitor afterward. Suddenly, her Mom was there with her coat in hand, she helped Juliana into it and off they went to the hospital.

***

About ten thirty Tuesday morning Al, Michael's boss signaled him to turn off the giant caterpillar tractor he drove. Michael turned off the loud dusty machine and jumped down to see what Al wanted him for.

"I have a message for you," Al yelled and tried to make himself heard above the noise of the trucks and paving equipment that worked around them.

"Come to the trailer for a moment," Al instructed. He walked ahead of Michael as clouds of dust swirled around them. Michael banged some of the grit off his clothes and boots as he entered the trailer. Scott sat waiting for him and he wondered what this was about.

Al turned to Michael and began," I knew you would want Scott here when I gave you the news."

Michael gave Scott a very puzzled look. He had just got a promotion to caterpillar operator; he knew that couldn't be it. Scott just sat and grinned at him. He didn't give a clue what was to come.

"Mrs. Winslow just called Juliana had her baby this morning. A healthy baby boy," Al said, as he handed both men a cigar.

Michael plunked down into the nearest chair. Suddenly his legs just wouldn't hold him. Michael shook his head mystified. "How did this happen she isn't due yet." He said and stared down at the cigar in his hand.

Scott got up then and shook Michael's hand, patted him on the back and congratulated him. Al offered his congratulations and lit Michael's cigar in keeping with the age-old boy's club tradition of smoking a cigar to celebrate the birth of a baby. Michael just held it and waved it around as he came out of his stupor and started to ask questions.

"When did she have the baby?
"Shortly after ten this morning."
"Are they both ok?"
"Yes"
"How big was the baby?" Michael wanted to know.
"Seven pounds, I think she said."
"She said Juliana would rest and wanted to see you after work," Al told him
"Do you think you can keep your mind on your work," Scott teased him.
"Yea don't run any of my men over," said Al with a wink to Scott.
"Gee guys I don't know," Michael said and ashed the cigar he had no intentions of smoking. He still looked awestruck. Both men exchanged a glance and grinned.
"I can give you time off if you need it," Al offered.
"Oh no I'll be fine; work will help pass the time."
"Ok then let's get back to work."
Michael spent the rest of the day in a fog. He had a million questions and Juliana held all the answers.

CHAPTER THIRTEEN

Juliana had come through a rough eight hours. She had slept most of the afternoon away. The nurse helped her freshen up in the bathroom, and then she sat and waited for Michael to get off work and come and see her. She couldn't wait to show him the baby. He had blond hair and she hoped someday chocolate brown eyes just like her's. Her Mom said he looked just like Juliana at her birth. Things couldn't have turned out better she was on cloud nine or maybe even ten or eleven.

Michael knocked on the door jam and walked in with a beautiful bouquet of flowers. They were beautiful spring flowers grown in a greenhouse and flown in. Most of them were yellow Juliana's favorite color. He crossed the room and handed her the flowers and gave her a hug over the rail of the bed. Jimmy hovered in the doorway. When Juliana noticed him she motioned for him to come in. She gave him a big hug as he handed her a pretty blue bunny with big floppy ears. "Thanks, Uncle Jimmy," she said, letting him know where he would stand in the baby's life. Jimmy blushed and smiled gratefully.

Juliana called the nurse and asked if she would bring the baby. Because the baby came early, he stayed in the nursery while Juliana slept. Michael and Jimmy stood nervously and waited for the nurse to bring him. Michael quizzed Juliana on her labor and delivery while they waited. Then they heard the bassinette coming down the hall toward them. Jimmy, a typical teen, couldn't wait and met the nurse in the hall. Michael walked over and grabbed Juliana's hand as they waited. They could hear Jimmy in the hall. He proudly told anyone who passed by. "This is my nephew."

Michael and Juliana exchanged a grin. Then Jimmy wheeled the bassinette into the room with the nurse who followed and Michael got his first glimpse of Juliana's baby.

He looked so very small. He was all wrapped up in a warm flannel blanket. Michael's eyes immediately became moist. The most precious little human being looked up at him from his blue blanket. A wisp of blond hair peeked out from under the tiny blue cap he had on. Smoky blue baby eyes met his, and Michael was done. A popular classic country song says "you had me from hello" well this baby had Michael. A love beyond his previous experience overtook him and swelled in his chest. The nurse picked the baby up and handed it to Juliana. Michael watched as Jimmy went over to the bedside and cooed to the baby.

"What will you call him?" Jimmy wanted to know.

"Tyler James Winslow," she told him proudly.

"Would you like to hold him?" Juliana offered.

Jimmy backed away. "Nah, I might break him."

"Here Michael how about you," she offered.

Michael looked visibly nervous but he stepped up and let Juliana place the baby in his outstretched arms.

"Hi Tyler," he said barely above a whisper. Nothing had prepared him for the feelings that sprang up out of nowhere. To know this little being was a part of Juliana. He felt a feeling of protection over Juliana and this little guy. Any one coming at Juliana or Tyler would have to come through him from now on. His eyes had totally misted over, afraid of dropping the precious little bundle; he gave Tyler back to his mother. Juliana was in awe and gratitude for the acceptance she saw in Michael's eyes. Her heart glowed with happiness. Life would be all right. At least that is what she thought.

Life fell into a routine for Juliana after that. She came home with the baby. He slept in the cradle beside her bed in her room. They brought her grandmother's old rocker into her room so she could feed Tyler in privacy and comfort. She had cleared off her dresser and made padding so she could use it as a changing table. It seemed that Tyler spent his first days quietly. He ate, slept and had his diaper changed. Juliana caught catnaps when she could. Juliana found that to keep Tyler clean and dry and fed was a full-time job.

Every evening she bundled him up and took him over to Michael and Jimmy's. They would visit and spend time together. Life was sweet. Michael would discuss his latest plan for the orchard. Some nights Juliana would sit and help Jimmy with his homework. And some nights she would fall asleep exhausted on the couch while Michael and Jimmy played with the baby. About eleven Juliana and Tyler would head home and the boys would head to bed.

About this time Michael's Mother came home from rehab. A cab brought her home on a Wednesday afternoon. Jimmy was in school and Michael was at work so Juliana and the baby greeted her when she walked in the door. Mom was so surprised and delighted.

"Oh Juliana you didn't have to do this," she exclaimed when she saw the decorations they had put up the night before, welcome home in big bold letters.

"Do you like them? Your sons did this for you," Juliana told her. She waited while Mrs. Ardath took her coat off and set her bags down.

"Oh let me get my hands on that little angel," she said and reached for Tyler.

Juliana's heart swelled. Her son would have people in his life that would overlook her mistake and love him unconditionally.

"You look wonderful Mrs. Ardath how are you feeling?" Juliana asked and noticed that Janet had lost the unhealthy pallor and the bags under her eyes.

"I feel great. Ready to tackle life again."

"Well, you remember we're here for you." Janet nodded.

Juliana made tea and they chatted, while the baby slept in his stroller and they waited for the boys to come home. Janet burst with news that Barry had asked if he could continue to see her. Juliana was happy for her, maybe he was just what she needed to make a fresh start.

***

The days clicked by in happy succession; Michael and Juliana saw each other almost every day. Little Tyler thrived. Janet attended AA meetings and stayed sober. Marion and Harvey, despite the embarrassment in public, enjoyed little Tyler.

All was fine until one night when instead of going to the Ardath's with the baby; Juliana had asked Michael to come over to her house for the evening. Tyler had a cold and she didn't want to take him out in the damp night air. Michael arrived about seven o'clock. Juliana met him at the back door and let him in. She gave him a big hug and then they headed into the living room where Tyler played with a mobile rigged over his playpen. Harvey sat and read his paper and Marion was there knitting. Juliana and Michael took a seat on the couch together.

"Juliana tells us you are fixing your fathers apple orchard," Harvey began.

"Yes, my brother Jimmy is helping me. We've studied my dad's old books. There's a lot to learn," Michael explained.

"When your father was alive it was a very viable business. Too bad it became run down," said Harvey and gave him a condemning look.

Michael sat and tried to assimilate that comment. He guessed Harvey referred to his stint in prison and his mother's neglect through her drinking. It hurt. It hurt a lot. Michael tried to give him the benefit of the doubt and when on.

"Jimmy and I have been able to save enough for a new brand of fertilizer that I am told will give it a boost."

"What shape is your dad's old sprayer in? It has to be on its last legs." Harvey asked next.

Would this man belittle and berate everything, Michael wondered.

"I've tried my best to recondition it sir," Michael told him a hint of annoyance in his voice.

The baby began to fuss then, and Juliana picked him up out of his designer playpen. She announced that he needed changing and left the room with him. Marion asked if they would like a cup of tea. Harvey said yes, and she left to go and make some.

Left alone the two men sat in awkward silence. Harvey stared across the room at Michael a now openly hostile look on his face. Michael glanced away at the fireplace and tried not to become more annoyed that he already was.

"What are doing hanging around my daughter?" Harvey asked. He drilled Michael with his hostile eyes.

When he recovered momentarily, Michael said," I love your daughter sir."

Well that was obviously not what Harvey wanted to hear. In typical Harvey Winslow fashion he abruptly got up and left the room. Michael sat on the couch stunned. Feelings of embarrassment, rejection and indignation washed over Michael. Does he really dislike me that much, Michael wondered. Oh yes, he was about to find out just how much.

CHAPTER FOURTEEN

Somehow Michael made it through the rest of that night. He tried his best not to let on to Juliana and her Mom that anything had happened to upset him. He played with little Tyler when Juliana brought him back all clean, and he smelled of that special sweet baby smell. He drank the tea Mrs. Winslow had made and at ten thirty he made his get away. Discouraged and forlorn he trudged home. He tried not to hold his behavior against Harvey. After all, he was just reacting the way everyone in the community who thought him guilty of the robbery did. He felt struck down but God would not let it destroy him.

It wasn't until a few days later that Harvey's dislike of him hit him full bore in the guts.

Thursday night came and Juliana was late. She was always at the Ardath's by eight. And if she couldn't come for any reason she always called. Michael paced anxiously at the living room window. When eight thirty came and she still hadn't come or called, he called her. She answered the phone on the fourth ring. "Hi Jewel's is everything ok, I thought you would be here by now."

"How could you Michael I never want to see you again." She said, tears in her voice.

"What?" he asked, flabbergasted.

"You know what you've done, don't try to act innocent with me," she cried.

"Juliana I have no idea what you are talking about," Michael told her and pleaded for understanding.

"My father saw you, you creep," she hurled at him.

"Saw what?" Michael asked. He tried to make some form of sense out of what she said.

"Saw you make out with Mandy Parsons," she cried, and the line went dead.

What on earth, thought Michael, he hadn't even seen Mandy Parsons since he had been back in town. But everyone in town knew her character. She was the town tramp. She hung out at the bars in town and would go home with almost anyone who asked. She had a child a couple of years back and a spinster woman in town had adopted the boy and was raising him.

How could Harvey think he had seen me with her? Michael wondered. He must have a serious eyesight problem. Michael would have laughed but this wasn't funny. Michael felt devastated, all of his wonderful future plans over in one mistaken identity.

Michael did what he could think of to try to fix things. Juliana refused to take his calls. When he walked over to her house, her parents met him at the door and headed him off. He asked Jimmy if he could talk to Juliana or her parents and try to make sense of it. But that didn't work either.

Michael felt devastated, even the day of his sentencing to prison, for something he had not done, wasn't worse than this.

He missed Tyler. He missed Juliana.

Then at work a couple of weeks later it came to him. Harvey had made it all up. He had to have made it all up. He asked Scott to find out if Mandy Parsons was in town.

***

Juliana felt beyond grief after her father told her what he had seen with his own eyes.

"Mom, I can't believe Michael would do such a thing."

"Well I know dear, and with that woman of all people," Marion sat with Juliana and tried to console her.

"Mom I love him, we want to get married one day."

"I know dear but maybe this is all for the best."

"How can you say that Mom," Juliana said as another set of sobs racked her.

Juliana tried to move through the following days. Tyler was a great comfort to her. She spent hours cooing to him, and she talked to him. Her heart felt broken and she felt she would never be the same. Some of the people at church were good to her and some treated her with distain and shunned her which she fully expected. It didn't help that it happened now when she was in a black funk. Her Mom tried her best to keep her busy but even she had begun to worry. Juliana had lost weight and lost interest in life in general.

***

Michael was in worse shape. Frustrated and inconsolable, he could not understand why this had happened. He felt he had done nothing to deserve this. Scott had no luck tracking down Mandy Parsons. He felt like his chance at a happy life disappeared, ripped out from under him. Nothing anyone said to him helped. He didn't sleep, and he didn't eat. He went to work in a fog and Al and Scott both kept an eye on him. They were afraid his inattention would cause him to be in a work related accident. Jimmy had tried so many times to talk to the Winslow's with no results. Forced to stop, it had come to the point where they threatened dismissal; he had pestered them so much.

Michael spent his weekends chasing leads. Scott helped a lot. He would get a lead on Friday night in the bar of where Mandy might be. Then the two of them would head off on Saturday morning to see if they could find her.

Sometimes Jimmy would tag along but it was always the same, either she had moved on or it was a false lead. Michael concluded it was hopeless and his life would have to go on longing for Juliana and Tyler with no chance of reconciliation.

Until one day when Tyler was about six months old. Scott had given Michael a ride home from work as usual on a Friday. Scott had gone to the bar with a few of the boys after work to have a few brews.

Suddenly about an hour later Scott knocked on Michael's door.

"Hey, what's up?" Michael greeted him.

"Get your coat on, I think I found her," Scott said breathless.

"You're kidding me," was all Michael could think to say.

Michael's heart sped up as he dashed to the closet to get his jacket.

"You think you really found her?"

"Yes, come on." Scott said trying to hurry him.

"I won't be here for supper Mom." He yelled into the kitchen to his Mom. "Scott thinks he found Mandy," he explained.

His Mom came out of the kitchen wiping her hands on a tea towel. "Good luck guys," she said, as she walked to the door to close it behind them.

They both raced to the car and Scott spun gravel as they sped down the laneway to the highway.

"Where is she, man?" Michael wanted to know.

"Some guy says he just saw her in King City."

"Man that's a long way," Michael exclaimed.

"Yea but it will be worth it if we find her."

"Thanks, man," Michael said.

As they turned on to the highway Michael got one quick glimpse into the Winslow yard. Juliana crossed the yard with Tyler in her arms. Michael craned his neck as far around as he could to try to keep her in sight. Man, she is beautiful, he thought, as Scott gave it the gas and sped down the highway.

This is all for you Jewels, he whispered under his breath.

They found Mandy a couple of hours away in a small town. She waited tables in a café and she was on duty when they got there. They had to wait to speak to her as she was busy waiting tables. That wait seemed like a century to Michael. Everything rode on her willingness to come back with them and explain to Juliana that she had never been with Michael.

She was his only chance to convince Juliana that he had not done something wrong. She was his only chance to get the life he wanted back. He prayed as hard as he knew how. In the end it was worth the wait as Mandy agreed to go back with them the following day to explain everything to Juliana.

That night Scott and Michael got a hotel room and had to wait until the following day when Mandy was ready to go with them. Michael had called home and told Jimmy of his plans and asked him to make sure Juliana would be home the next day. "And what ever you do, don't let her Mom or Dad know that I will see her," Michael insisted.

"Ok, bro, I'll make sure. Oh, and good luck," Jimmy said signing off.

The next day was a bright sunny day. It was a perfect day for a long drive. But none of the passengers in Scott's car cared about the weather or a leisurely drive. The car sped across the blacktop at just above the speed limit. Butterflies chased one another around in Michael's stomach. He had not been this nervous in a very long time. After what felt like forever, they finally pulled into Michael's driveway. As soon as Jimmy heard the car he was out the door.

"Is she going to see me?" asked Michael, afraid of what the answer might be.

"Yes, I am to call and she will come right over," Jimmy explained.

They all went in the house and settled in the living room. Jimmy made the call and they all sat and waited for Juliana to arrive.

Fifteen minutes seemed like an hour to Michael. He sat nervously biting his lip and tried to pray. Not one coherent thought would come and finally he just said. "Thy will be done, Lord."

***

Juliana had been miserable for so long, all she wanted was for everything to be back the way it was before her Dad told her about seeing Michael and Mandy together. She felt so sad and so betrayed. This last while had been the hardest time of her young life. She knew now that she loved Michael with all of her heart, but she just could not forgive what he had done. Jimmy had called and said that Michael now had proof that he had not been with Mandy. She had waited all-day for Jimmy to call and say they were ready for her to come over. She left Tyler with her Mother and let on she went out for a walk. Her stomach was upset as she walked the short distance to the Ardath's front door. She took a deep breath and knocked.

Jimmy opened the door and welcomed her in. He took her coat and hung it up. As she walked further into the living room, Scott was the first person she saw. He smiled and she smiled back. Then she spied Mandy and she stopped, completely taken aback.

Mandy got to her feet and Juliana took a step backward. Jimmy quickly stepped forward. She noticed Michael then; he sat further back in a corner. He gave her a pleading look.

Jimmy spoke," Juliana, you remember Mandy."

"Yes," said Juliana feeling shaken.

"Juliana, Michael and Scott came and found me and told me what happened. About your Dad saying he had seen Michael and I together. Juliana, Michael never comes in the bar, and I have never been with him in a car or anywhere. I can't figure out what your dad could be talking about," said Mandy.

Suddenly, Juliana took a seat on the vacated couch. Her legs were about to give out. Mandy sat down on the couch with her and looked directly into Juliana's face. Juliana sat for a few moments and tried to take in what Mandy told her.

Juliana had known Mandy since high school. Mandy had always been wild and loose. Juliana knew her home situation had never been a good one. Juliana knew Mandy, and she knew she had the reputation as the town tramp, and that might be true. But she also knew Mandy was not a liar. Many events had happened during high school, but Mandy had always told the truth.

"So you're telling me that you where not in a car with Michael, and you have never made out with him."

"That's right," said Mandy, keeping her gaze fixed on Juliana's face.

She shook her head then and searched the room for Michael. "This is what you tried to tell me all along."

Michael stood up and nodded and gave her the slightest of smiles.

A second later, she was off the couch and in Michael's arms. Both cried now. The others in the room gave one another high fives. Juliana's heart floated somewhere near the ceiling, she was so happy. Michael felt so relieved. A miracle happened, they found Mandy and Juliana had believed her. Now, he just wanted to see Tyler. They decided though that they had better wait until tomorrow for that because Juliana now had to go and face her father and mother. She would have to determine whether it was a case of mistaken identity or if her father had lied to her.

Mandy could not remember being in a car with any men so they all suspected it had been a lie made up to keep them apart.

Tyler played in his playpen when Juliana got home. She took him and changed him and then sat down with her parents to discuss what had happened.

In the end Harvey had to admit he had concocted a lie to keep Michael out of his daughter's life. Marion was aghast and ashamed that her husband would do such a thing.

Juliana explained to her dad how much she cared for Michael and that she wanted to be with him.

Her father admitted that he had come to realize that she truly loved Michael these last few months. But he felt the lie had taken on a life of its own, and he hadn't known how to take it back.

He vowed to his wife and daughter that he had learned a lesson, and he would never try anything like that again.

***

Juliana awoke a few months later, a beautiful June morning and Tyler stood up in his crib across the room from her. She knew he probably needed a diaper changed, but she played peek-a-boo for a couple of minutes before she got up to look after him. He giggled and smiled as his mother's face disappeared under her quilt. Life was good once again. She would marry Michael later today. Juliana and her Mom had sent out numerous invitations to relatives and friends. Many had declined to come. It was hurtful, but Juliana understood that some people still felt Michael was guilty, and some couldn't forgive her lapse in judgment. Bur her parents and her Aunt Joe would be there, and some friends from the church, and the guys from Michael's construction would all be there. Her dad would walk her down the aisle, and her Mom would walk behind them carrying Tyler in a tux that matched the one Michael had rented for the day.

***

Chaos abounded at the Ardath house. Scott, Michael and Jimmy all tried to get ready for the wedding. Jimmy couldn't find his good shoes. Michael couldn't find the cuff links that were suppose to come with the tux. Janet helped Barry pin on a boutonniere. He was now the step dad to be of the groom. Scott panicked because it was his job to get the groom there on time and it didn't look like that would happen. Janet helped Barry, then went to find an old pair of cuff links that had belonged to Michael's father. Michael's eyes misted as Janet helped put them through the cuffs of his shirt. Jimmy finally found his dress shoes and all was well. Scott took the boys in his car and Barry and Janet came in her car.

Michael stood at the front of the church. His month had gone dry. And he was sure even his knees were sweating. His heart, beat an irregular rhythm in his chest. Scott, his best man, sensed his nervousness and briefly hugged his shoulders with one arm. Jimmy stood beside Scott and nervously put his hand in his pocket every couple of seconds. Michael wanted him to be the one to hand him the ring and he kept making sure it was still there. The fragrance of roses spread all through the church. There where yellow roses everywhere. There were sprays at the end of each pew. Two huge bouquets stood at the front of the church. Babies breathe and fern fronds interlaced in the bouquets. Michael spied Juliana's Aunt Josephine in the congregation. She had Sparky, her little dog ,with her in her lap. Aunt Joe caught Michael's eye and winked. Michael couldn't help but wink back. He had met Aunt Joe last night at the rehearsal party, and he had fallen in love with the elderly woman. He determined they would make many trips to include her in their new formed family.

The organist stopped playing and now struck the first chords of the wedding march.

All eyes turned to the back of the church. Juliana stood beside her father in a dress that Scarlet O'Hara would have envied. It was a champagne color with hoops under it. Seed pearls graced the bodice in an intricate pattern. Long Italian lace sleeves came to a point over the back of her hands. The skirt of the dress almost filled the aisle. And the train flowed in scallops of lace behind her. A small diamond tiara held a veil of multiple layers in place. Seed pearls graced its edges. Michael gasped aloud at the sight. Scott poked him in the back.

Two of Juliana's nursing school friends were bridesmaids. Juliana and her Dad started down the aisle in perfect time to the music. Her Mom, with Tyler in her arms came along at a distance behind the train.

As she came down the aisle, Juliana smiled at the friends that had come to celebrate this happy occasion with her. There was Manuel and his wife, she barely recognized him in a suit. Even Mandy had come. She was the reason they were finally able to be together, they both agreed she deserved to be there today.

The happy couple would go away for a few days honeymoon. Marion would keep Tyler until they got back. While they were away, Janet would move out and go to live in the same small town as Barry. So Michael and Juliana, Tyler and Jimmy would make a new family at the Ardath's farm.

The minister finished the ceremony and just as he said, "May I now present to you Mr. and Mrs. Michael Ardath." Aunt Joe's little Sparky jumped off her knee and ran up to Juliana.

The little white ball of fur pawed at Juliana's dress wanting her attention. The congregation all laughed as Juliana and Michael bent down and both got doggie kisses on their cheeks.

Bubbles filled the sanctuary as the happy couple walked down the aisle, the little dog trotted along behind.

Proof

1720317

Made in the USA